W

NOV 0 1 2017

Death
and
Douglas

J.W. OCKER

Sky Pony Press
New York

First Edition

This is a work of fiction. Names, characters, places, and incidents are from the authors' imaginations, and used fictitiously.

Visit our website at www.skyponypress.com.

Books, authors, and more at www.skyponypressblog.com.

www.jwocker.com

10 9 8 7 6 5 4 3 2 1

Library of Congress Control Number: 2017950093

Cover illustration by Lisa K. Webber
Cover design by Sammy Yuen

Hardcover ISBN: 978-1-5107-2457-0
Ebook ISBN 978-1-5107-2462-4

Printed in the United States of America

For Mom

RIP

Death
and
Douglas

September 10

Saturday

CHAPTER 1

A small black crow of a boy leaned against the roof of a dead man. The boy's features, where they were black, were extremely black, and where they were pale, extremely pale. A carefully combed slick of thick black hair defined his northern border, three parallel off-shoots of which angled across his forehead like they had been gouged there by the claw of a cat.

He placed his cheek against the cool, smooth sarcophagus lid, his arms lolling across it and obscuring the name inscribed on its surface. The boy seemed to be listening for sounds from the long-dead remains inside, but his pale green eyes were mesmerized by the magic that a pair of men were conjuring less than a hundred feet away, across a throng of granite gravestones and angels. It involved a large pile of dirt, a long polished box, and a deep rectangular hole with precisely cut corners.

One of the men, a tall, bearded clod of dirt dressed in three different shades of brown, was saying to the other, "A major difference between kids and grown-ups is what they think about the important subject of holes. Kids love holes, and dig them often and in as many places as they can. Smooth sandy beaches, flat dirt lots, glistening fields of snow, ladle-shaped mounds of mashed potatoes—there's nothing a kid hates more than an uninterrupted surface. Grown-ups, on the other hand, hate holes, and generally want them filled, flattened, and fixed out of existence. Potholes, sinkholes, holes in clothes, holes in theories, holes in emotional well-being . . . and they absolutely can't stand gophers. Sometimes, it seems as if the entire adult world is dedicated to plugging holes."

"Poor saps," grunted the other man, who was pulling himself out of the hole. He was younger and sported a long green coat and long brown hair.

The brown man continued. "Few grown-ups manage to preserve the wonder that something, and in fact most things, can be dug. Even fewer find themselves fortunate enough to make a career out of digging holes. Feaster, we are lucky men."

"Sure, Moss. And we have the blistered hands and aching backs to prove it."

They both stared proudly down into their hole. It was twice as long as it was wide, about as deep as a bunk bed was tall, and seemed to be created to the exact specifications of the nearby polished wooden box with brass handles.

"It is certainly a fine hole," said the man named Moss. "Wouldn't mind being tucked in there myself, if I do say so myself." He leaned against his shovel, which he'd planted firmly in the dirt like a flagpole.

"Sure. She'll love it, I think," agreed Feaster, taking off his hat and wiping his brow, which was sweaty despite the pre autumn chill on the air. He flicked an unsettlingly thick earthworm back into the hole with the toe of his boot and looked around, squinting. "Speaking of kids who love holes, where's Spadeful? Not like him to miss a planting."

Thus summoned, the small black crow of a boy tore off from his sarcophagus perch and popped his head around the giant pile of dirt that had formerly occupied Moss and Feaster's hole.

"Ah, ain't nothing sadder than a kid in a cemetery . . ." said Feaster.

"Unless that kid is alive," said Moss. "Nice tie."

Spadeful's real name was Douglas Mortimer. Only Moss and Feaster called him Spadeful. It was part of an ongoing joke that started when he was much smaller about how much dirt they'd need to fill his grave. Douglas was twelve years old, but still small for his age. It didn't help matters that he was wearing a serious-looking black suit that was a tad too big, out of which peeked a little yellow beak of a tie.

"Sorry I'm late. Had to wait for Mom to drop me off. She wouldn't let me walk over by myself."

Douglas visited the cemetery almost every day. According to the plaque on the black iron gates at its entrance, the cemetery had been established in 1644. It was a year so far back, that for a long time Douglas had thought the number was the cemetery's address. Inside, five hundred acres of hilly property stretched to the end of the earth as far as Douglas knew. Large mausoleums sprang from gentle hills, life-sized statues writhed in grief, tombstones sprouted in hundreds of different shapes, their eloquent epitaphs discussing eternity together. A cold stream cut a thin Styx through the back of the cemetery, where it was more forest than cemetery. Over that stream was a covered bridge where Douglas would play "Headless Horseman" when he wasn't racing through the stones or searching for epitaphs that included his name.

"What's wrong with Daisy today?" Douglas nodded at the monstrosity behind the two men.

Daisy was a large, yellow contraption that looked like a cross between all the horrible parts of a spider and all the terrible parts of a scorpion. It had originally started out as a simple backhoe loader. A bucket and arm in the rear to dig holes, a loader in the front to fill them back in. Over the years, the two men had adapted this tractor to fit the needs of the cemetery, which amounted to more than digging and filling. Now, Daisy could carry grave vaults, lower caskets, seed and mow grass, install headstones, and do anything one needed for the dead, with the exception of maybe resurrecting them. The only downside to all their tinkering was that Daisy's various mechanisms only worked about fifty percent of the time. That was why both men were now digging the grave by hand while Daisy propped up their backsides when they got tired.

"Don't know. I think she decided that we should dig this beauty the old-fashioned way," replied Moss.

"It's good for us gravediggers to do that every once in a while," added Feaster, who always smelled like cloves even when covered in dirt and sweat. "Else we'd never get to use the symbol of our office." He grabbed his shovel and held it blade-up like a scepter.

"If I were a younger man, I'd agree. Since I'm not, you can take the symbol of our office"—Moss glanced at Douglas—"and dig your own grave." He stuck both hands in the small of his back and arched himself until a violent series of cracks broke the solemn stillness of the cemetery. Douglas imagined the dead below, annoyed and mumbling to themselves before turning over in their caskets.

"Is this Mrs. Laurent?" Douglas pointed a finger at the wooden box while plopping himself down on the ground, his feet dangling off the edge of the hole like he was sitting on a dock.

"In person," said one.

"In coffin," said the other.

Douglas looked down into the hole. The grave was empty except for the open concrete grave liner, which was in place to hold the coffin and keep the earth from caving in when the coffin eventually decayed. Douglas saw the tail end of a prehistorically large earthworm squeezing itself through one of the drainage holes in the bottom of the liner.

"Can I see her?"

Moss squinted at Douglas, while Feaster yelped, "What?"

"Can I see her?"

"I guess," said Feaster after a few seconds. He stretched his shoulders blades back until they almost touched and then stepped toward the coffin.

"Wait a minute there, sir." Moss lifted a finger at Feaster and then turned to Douglas. "I know you're just being curious, but I don't think that would be a good idea, Spadeful."

"Why?" asked Douglas. Feaster wrinkled his forehead at Moss, and the two earth-toned men exchanged a glance aimed over Douglas's head. Then the two slowly opened a pair of mirrored grins that seemed, had they been sewn together, to stretch farther than the width of their faces combined.

Moss made a show of looking over his shoulder, and leaned closer to Douglas, using his shovel as a pivot. "It's because, after she died, they discovered that she was a gorgon." Feaster nodded beside him in what was either agreement or approval.

"What's a gorgon?"

"Oh, it's a fiendish beast, looks like a woman, but has snakes for hair and a forked tongue . . . well worth staying away from. If you see her face, even in death, you'll turn into a stone fit to sit at the head of a grave."

"They didn't even open the casket for the funeral," added Feaster. "Would have wrecked the whole thing, all those mourners gathered around suddenly becoming statues."

Douglas smiled wide, and with two hands, pulled a pile of the moist, newly dug grave dirt toward him, which he started shaping into a castle. "Mom gets annoyed by your stories. She says you're arresting my development or something."

Moss swatted the notion away with a calloused hand. "Gah, if it weren't for us, people like your mother would have to deal with the monster themselves. Heck, without us, the whole town of Cowlmouth would be overrun by them."

"We're very important to what you might call the ecosystem of the town," explained Feaster. "We maintain Cowlmouth's equilibrium."

"That means *balance*," translated Moss.

"Man and monster must live together, according to a very strict ratio. If it weren't for the work we do right in this here rot garden"—Feaster stabbed the earth a few times with the blade of his shovel—"who knows what would happen?"

"It wouldn't be good," said Moss.

"Somebody needs to keep the dead down," said Feaster.

"Someone needs to stake the hearts of the vampires when they rise from their crypts," Moss added.

"Somebody needs to bash the brains out of the zombies when they claw their way back through the earth."

"Somebody needs to shove the cackling curses of witches back into their toothless mouths."

"Somebody needs to appease the plights of restless spirits."

"Ghosts, the poor wretches. Sometimes, they just need a little direction."

Despite his mother's cautions, Douglas was hooked, as he always was. He loved their stories of monsters, even if he didn't believe them. Not really, anyway. Plus, if it weren't for Moss and Feaster, Douglas wouldn't have banshees and ifrits and gorgons, or any other exotic types of monster, to run wild in his imagination. And an imagination needed its monsters. Still, he couldn't be too much of a kid about it in front of them.

"I've never seen any."

Moss leaned closer to Douglas, the pivot of his shovel bending almost horizontal, his face deadly serious. "That's a good thing, Spadeful. But there are monsters. You can bet your child-sized soul on that."

A ragged howl ripped across the cemetery.

CHAPTER 2

Moss and Feaster jumped to their feet, shovels at the ready, swiveling back and forth like they were baseball batters who couldn't find the pitcher.

The howl quickly broke into high-pitched laughter as an angular silhouette stepped in front of the cemetery gates and pinched its face between the bars. "Moss! Feaster!" the form yelled. "Watch out for monsters!"

"That boy," said Moss. "That demon boy."

Douglas let out his own laugh and gave a goodbye salute to the two gravediggers. He leapfrogged tombstones until he got to the gate, where the thin form was still quaking with laughter. If Douglas was a crow of a boy, then Lowell Pumphrey was his pal scarecrow.

Lowell was a year older than Douglas, a year wiser, a year dumber, and almost fourteen according to Lowell, but that was just another way of saying thirteen. He was thin and tall, with wrists and ankles escaping in terror from the long sleeves of his orange sweatshirt and the legs of his jeans. Atop his head was a campfire of yellow, curly hair that looked like an anemone sifting the air for food. Douglas didn't have a lot of friends, but a lot of friends for Lowell Pumphrey was a good trade.

"I was just at your house," said Lowell.

"What were you doing there?"

"Eating your dinner."

"Um . . ."

"I mean, I didn't go there to eat, but you weren't there, and your mom offered, so I thought, 'What the hockey sticks?' So how come you're here? I mean, besides the fact that you're almost always here."

"I wanted to see Mrs. Laurent get buried. Moss and Feaster said she was a gorgon."

"Awesome. Speaking of that, I was looking for you because I have big news. This town is about to get crazy."

"Why?"

"You'll like this. There's a monster. In town. And not this Halloween stuff that Moss and Feaster feed you.

I'm talking the kind of monster that would make those guys cower in their grave holes."

"What do you mean?"

"I don't have time now, man. I spent it all eating your mom's chop suey. Tomorrow, though, let's meet back here." Lowell looked around to make sure that nobody was nearby. "It's the kind of news that we don't want any coffee-drinkers to overhear."

"Tomorrow is Mr. Stauffer's funeral."

"Oh, yeah. I'm going to that, too. Afterwards, then. Anyway, gotta go. Second dinnertime. Dad's making meatballs." Lowell grabbed Douglas by the arms. "Round meat!"

"Sure. See you—"

Before he could finish the goodbye, Lowell bolted away, eating up the sidewalk with his long strides and taking mere seconds before he was little more than a tiny figure in the distance. Douglas could just make out his friend's upraised arms and barely heard his battle cry of "Meatballs!" wafting behind him. In like a lion, out like a lion. That was Lowell Pumphrey.

Cowlmouth Cemetery wasn't too far from Douglas's house. Everywhere that Douglas went wasn't too far from his house. The town of Cowlmouth was large enough as far as towns went in New England, but Douglas only really went to a few places. His house, the cemetery, school, Lowell's house, the movie theater, the ice cream shop, all of which were within a few streets of one another.

A few streets are universe enough for a twelve-year-old boy, and close enough to it for everybody else.

As Douglas meandered home from the cemetery, he swished a white twig that he'd plucked from an obliging birch tree along the way. It glided back and forth in front of him like a harvesting scythe. Around him, Cowlmouth was starting to kindle its autumn fires. It was still early September, and only a few impatient trees lifted a red- or yellow-flaming torch in the midst of their mostly green branches. In another few weeks, every birch, every elm, and every oak would be in full five-alarm conflagration before finally fading to brown and being buried under snow for the winter.

Today, he didn't notice the shifting of seasons too much, though. Douglas Mortimer was as worried as a boy could be, not having had much practice at it so far in life. His mother and father had changed in the past week or two—gotten busier, maybe. They weren't around to see him as much. And he didn't understand it. His parents worked from home—Douglas under-stood that part—but lately, it was as if they not only didn't notice him, but didn't want him to notice them.

But it wasn't just them. It was other adults, too. Like Dr. Coffman, the family doctor. Douglas didn't know how old Dr. Coffman was, but he always thought him to be the oldest person he had ever seen. White wispy hair on his head, white bristly hair on his cheeks, a cadaverously thin frame. His ears and nostrils were plugged with white hairs, as well, as if his head were full of the richest soil a growing thing could want. The other day, the doctor had dropped by Douglas's house. He didn't even say hi to Douglas or offer any of the lemon candy that he always had on him. The kind that Douglas didn't really like, but liked getting all the same. Dr. Coffman had nodded absentmindedly at him before Douglas's parents had shooed Douglas out of the room. His parents weren't normally ones to shoo.

By the time he arrived home, Lowell's bluster had almost blown away his troubling thoughts. Douglas couldn't even begin to guess what kind of monster Lowell had been talking about, but judging by the look in his friend's eyes, it was exciting.

Douglas paused in front of his house. He remembered that his mother had made him promise to have Moss or Feaster give him a lift home. Hopefully, she wouldn't ask. Besides, he wasn't even sure if the grave-diggers were allowed to cross the borders of the cemetery. Seemed like it was the only place he ever saw them. His mother's request was weird, anyway. He'd walked to and from the cemetery by himself hundreds of times.

Douglas's house was a towering construct, paneled and painted a somber forest green, with dark purple shutters and a black roof. The house was old, large, and sprawling, with two big towers like the eye stalks of a snail, and so many pointy gables and dormers that it looked like the architect didn't know how to draw a straight line. A wide, dark green sign with gold lettering in a comforting script was staked on two granite posts into the front lawn. It read MORTIMER FAMILY FUNERAL HOME.

It was his family. And his home.

Home sweet funeral home.

SEPTEMBER 11

SUNDAY

CHAPTER

3

Douglas Mortimer had come to grips with death at an early age: birth.

It's bound to happen when one's parents run a funeral home, and it's bound and gagged to happen when one's parents are the third generation to do so. Douglas's first memory was of the dead. He recalled his father lifting him up over the lip of a coffin so that he could touch the body inside. He couldn't have been more than three at the time, and the only impression that stuck with him from the experience was the heat of his father's hands beneath his armpits.

That was why Douglas felt right at home beneath the gigantic dying Jesus at the back of the auditorium of Cowlmouth Center Church, handing out funeral programs to mourners lining up in the foyer for the Stauffer funeral. Up front, the organ groaned out a dirge that he had heard enough times that he almost found it catchy.

Cowlmouth Center Church was a vast establishment. Dark rib-like beams buttressed a sweeping white ceiling over soft red carpeting that matched the upholstered wooden pews. The pulpit on the dais at the front was a massive piece of dark furniture that almost eclipsed the tiered choir loft behind it. Backdropping both the pulpit and the choir loft was an enormous round stained glass window with an abstract pattern of mostly blue, red, and white panels that made whoever stood at the pulpit look like the pupil in a giant eye. At the back of the church, on both sides of the oversized dying Jesus, was a pair of balconies that almost doubled the seating capacity of the place of worship.

That was how the church always looked, but today, at the foot of the pulpit, another massive piece of wooden furniture dominated the holy place—the coffin of Irwin Stauffer. Leaning in apparent inconsolable grief against the side of the coffin was a large, white sign with red lettering that proclaimed: HOT DOGS: $2.50.

Below the price was a cartoon drawing of a tube of meat with wide eyes and an outstretched tongue.

Irwin Stauffer had been a popular man in Cowlmouth, which was why his funeral had to be held at the largest church in town. All it took to secure that pre-death fame and post-death regard was a small red-and-white-striped cart laden with hot dogs, near the town square. Mr. Stauffer had parked his little cart there every summer for sixty years and was as much a fixture of the town as the old library or the massive bronze statue of its colonial founder that stood guard in front of the town hall. He always boasted that he had sold a hot dog to "darn near everybody in this town at one time or another, even the vegetarians." It was rumored that plans were now in the works to name the square after him.

"Your dad wanted me to find out if you were all set for programs." Christopher Shin was a tall Korean man in his early twenties. The individual hairs of his thin moustache seemed to each be separated by half an inch of bald skin, and his blue-striped tie was held in place by a gold-plated bar that matched a pair of cuff links holding his sleeve-ends together. On his suit lapel was a green and gold Mortimer Family Funeral Home name tag that matched the one on Douglas's own lapel.

Christopher was the Mortimer Family Funeral Home apprentice, which meant he was learning the trade the hard way, answering midnight calls for corpse removals, picking up flowers, and doing all the little jobs that it takes to eventually get a body six feet under the ground. Like Douglas, he lived at the funeral home, but unlike Douglas, he had chosen this lifestyle. Douglas never could figure out why. Christopher often acted as if the people who died in this town did so simply to overload him with work.

"I got plenty." He motioned at the four boxes on the table behind him.

"Good. You'll need them. A lot of people are coming. It's going to be a real hassle." Christopher moved off to tackle whatever next duty was going to decrease the quality of his life.

"Hi, Douglas. That's a nice tie." It was Chief Pumphrey, Lowell's father. Lowell and his kid brother, Josh, were behind him. Douglas's tie was dark green with scallop shapes that made it look like a scaly lizard seeking shelter in his dark blue blazer.

"Thanks." Douglas handed Lowell's father a funeral program. On the front was a painting of Mr. Stauffer in his trademark straw boater hat and red suspenders, beaming from behind his hot dog cart, a mustard-smeared hot dog in one hand and a ketchup-smeared one in the other. The original painting had hung in a corridor at the town hall for at least a decade.

Lowell passed Douglas, turned down a program, gave him a bump on the shoulder with a sideways fist, and tapped two fingers on the side of his nose before passing him wordlessly to find a place to sit. Douglas heard the message like it had been shouted: "Don't forget about the cemetery afterwards . . . a real-life monster . . . and your tie isn't that nice."

Before Douglas had too much time to wonder again about the monster, a small hand missing one of its fingers eagerly thrust itself forward for a program. The man with only nine fingers was short. Like almost Douglas's height. He was also rather meaty for his size, which explained the slight skim of sweat that formed on the bridge of his nose and made his thick curly brown hair droop in damp bunches like Spanish moss around his head. The bottom half of his face had a perpetual fuzz of stubble, and the top half was punctured with two deep-set, dark brown eyes. One of them winked at Douglas.

"How do I smell, Douglas?"

Douglas took a whiff. "You smell like leather. And formaldehyde."

"New cologne." Eddie Brunswick worked for the Mortimer family as an embalmer, and he was on an ongoing quest to cover up what he did for a living. That meant the smell and the stains. As a result, Eddie was an expert on colognes and detergents. He hadn't yet succeeded in his mission, but he could name just about any scent at twenty paces and could work wizardry with a washing machine. After receiving his program, Eddie took a step inside and spent a few seconds of intense deliberation as he scoped out the attendees. He chose an open seat on the pew beside the nearest pretty girl he could find. The girl scooted away, closer to her boyfriend, who sat on her other side.

The line to get into the auditorium was starting to back up, so Douglas began handing out programs as fast as he could, regularly diving into the cardboard boxes on the table to get more when he ran out. Fortunately, he had already claimed one of the programs for his own personal collection. It rested in his inside jacket pocket, beside his scaly tie.

Soon his rhythm of handing out programs grew so flawless that he hardly stopped to acknowledge the people he knew or to ineffectually brush the stiff, shiny strands of black hair on his forehead back into place. He was halfway through a second box of programs when the girl happened.

He didn't have much time to observe her, as she was gone before he'd realized he'd handed her a program. All he retained was a vague afterimage of long, black hair and a flash of purple. But it had been enough time to interrupt his pace. The pause must have dragged on a bit too long; an ugly snort startled his attention back to the line of mourners.

"Hrmph."

A tall woman wearing thick-framed glasses and a dark dress dotted with flowers so small they appeared as though they were being sucked into a void towered over him. Douglas's face turned the color of the church carpet, and he quickly handed her a program.

As soon as the stream of funeral attendees ended, Douglas put the box of remaining programs under the table and made his way deeper into the church. Normally, he would sit in the back so he could hold the door for the pallbearers at the end of the service. His place was always saved at Mortimer Family funerals. The only other person who could say that was the deceased, and they couldn't actually say that. His parents, on the other hand, rarely could be found in one place, much less sitting during the funerals they arranged. Instead they hovered on the edges, ready to make sure that everything went smoothly for the bereaved.

Douglas saw his father in a side aisle moving a large arrangement of flowers out of the way to allow a group easier access to a pew. He nodded solemnly at Douglas across the crowd before focusing his attention back on the funeral. Mr. Mortimer was of medium height, with fine black hair, pale skin, and a general tautness to his features. Douglas had inherited most of his own physical characteristics from him. Douglas couldn't see his mother, but was sure she was attending to the less visible parts of the funeral—calling the cemetery to ensure that everything was prepared, planning cleanup, or checking with the police assigned to direct the long procession that would be slithering its way across town in the next hour.

Instead of taking his place near the doors, Douglas walked along the back wall of the auditorium to the stairs that led to the left-hand balcony. On his way, he passed Lowell's father talking quietly to Dr. Coffman.

"I feel terrible for thinking it, especially at his funeral, but Irwin's death couldn't have been better timed." That was Chief Pumphrey.

"I assume you mean because it's distracting everyone from the . . . untimely death of Mrs. Laurent?" returned Dr. Coffman.

"Exactly."

"Man always did put the town first."

Douglas barely registered the name of the woman Moss and Feaster had called a "gorgon." He ascended the stairs, and without even looking around, walked to the very last row of the large gallery and took an empty seat in the back corner. His nearest neighbor was the giant head of Jesus rearing up beside him like a Titan rising from the sea. He scanned the crowd in the balcony, searching for the dark-haired girl. She was five rows in front of him. All he could see of her was the back of her head, but he scrutinized that sleek veil of black hair like someone peering into a fresh night sky waiting for the stars to come out.

The organ abruptly cut off in the middle of one of its sadder chords and a man in black religious attire walked to the pulpit above the prone Mr. Stauffer. Like the coffin and the pulpit, Revered Ahlgrim and Mr. Stauffer now formed a set of perpendicular lines. Douglas knew the reverend well, as his family had worked with him longer than Douglas had been alive. He was a very round man. His stomach was round. The lenses of his spectacles were round. His bald head was round. Even the way he formed his words was round. He was like a snowman. In fact, the only angles on him were the four that formed the golden crucifix around his neck.

From this angle and at this distance, Douglas saw Mr. Stauffer's still face as an indistinct flesh-colored oval against the light satin of the coffin interior. Douglas had seen him back at the funeral home. Mr. Stauffer had fewer wrinkles than he should have for his age, and a loose head of hair that had wilted to gray. His final expression was as though he were listening to his favorite music on headphones. As usual, Eddie had done good work.

Reverend Ahlgrim began the service. "Good morning, fellow mourners." Douglas could hear every "o" in that opening address. "Irwin Stauffer was a man made of summer. The season didn't officially start here in Cowlmouth until Irwin sold his first hot dog. Unfortunately, as we leave this last summer and pass into fall, Irwin passes, too . . ."

So far, the service was an excellent one in Douglas's opinion. And his opinion mattered because he'd been to many funerals. Mr. Stauffer looked great, the flowers looked great, the turnout was great, and even Reverend Ahlgrim's eulogy was great, full of comforting words.

However, even at their best, Douglas had always been slightly dissatisfied with funerals. For him, death was a regular event. It was a time for people to gather together, just the same as Christmas, a birthday, or the Fourth of July, as inevitable as Wednesday following Tuesday, March following February. Every sentence has a punctuation mark. Everybody gets a year older until they don't. Everybody dies.

He thought that funerals should be merrier. Instead of blowing into tissues, attendees should be blowing into party favors. Eulogies should be accompanied by toasts. Mourners should wear party hats instead of veils. The silk-lined boxes should be treated with the same anticipation as paper-wrapped ones.

Eventually, the funeral ended, and the organ below resurrected itself with a moan like the grim realization of a school morning. Seven pallbearers, including the mayor and Chief Pumphrey, approached the coffin. Douglas's father closed the lid with a gentle and practiced motion, and six of them reverently picked up Mr. Stauffer and walked down the aisle. The seventh grabbed the hot dog sign and held it in front of him like a flag at a state procession. After a few moments in which the remaining members of the Stauffer family left the front rows and followed the pallbearers out to the awaiting hearse, the rest of the attendees began to shuffle out of their rows to leave the church.

Douglas stayed glued in place, secretly investigating the profile of the dark-haired girl as she walked toward the aisle. She was as pale as birch bark, with delicate features and a slight awkwardness to her walk. On her hand—the hand that held the very program he had given her—was a large, purple stone set in silver. Her black dress had bits of red lint on it from the pew.

She looked back in his direction.

It was just a glance, one that might have been random or intended for the giant Christ head that peeked over Douglas's shoulder, but it gave him a sense of vertigo, like he was on an elevator descending too fast.

Before he knew it, she'd disappeared down the stairs.

Outside, Mr. Stauffer was being loaded into the Mortimer Family Funeral Home hearse, which would take him to a cemetery in nearby Osshua, the town where he was born. Moss and Feaster wouldn't get the honor of planting this man.

And while Mr. Stauffer might not be going to Cowlmouth Cemetery that afternoon, Douglas certainly was. He had to find out about Lowell's monster.

Preoccupied with that big news and the girl with the purple ring (but mostly the girl with the purple ring) Douglas leaped down the balcony steps three at a time, only to run right into a stare hard enough to almost knock the wind out him. Standing at the opposite side of the church was that same tall woman he'd handed a program to, boring holes into his skull through the magnifying lenses of her glasses. Her expression didn't seem to have changed at all in the past hour. Douglas headed toward the exit with a little more purpose, but turned his head one last time to look back at her. She was still glowering at him through those narrowed eyes, the tiny flowers on her dress still being eaten by the void.

CHAPTER
4

Douglas loved Cowlmouth Cemetery. It was his park, his backyard, his playground. It was a foundation for his imagination and a forum for all his big questions. His parents were okay with that. They didn't find it morbid. Or, more accurately, they found it morbid, but morbid means something totally different to morticians. Lowell and Douglas had passed many a day here in the old rot garden, as Feaster called it.

Today, the sky was clear, the sun bright, and the temperature comfortable. It was beautiful . . . which meant that it was a less-than-ideal day to visit a cemetery. Cemetery visits, Douglas believed, were best enjoyed when the weather was chilly, the sky was overcast, and nature itself seemed to be in mourning.

The gravestones Douglas and Lowell passed as they walked deeper into the graveyard seemed different, as if they sensed the approaching Halloween, that time of year when they would be most in season.

They eventually found themselves near a grave with a window. It marked the final earthly resting place of Harold Dumont, MD. The doctor had apparently been so afraid of being buried alive that he had designed his grave to ensure that it didn't happen. A horizontal stone was inset into the top of a knoll, with a small, thick pane of glass centered in the stone six feet above and directly over where Dr. Dumont's face was. Another capstone supposedly hid a stairwell that led directly into the grave. The story went that Dr. Dumont was buried with a bell in his hand and a breathing tube connecting his mouth to the surface, although Douglas had never been able to find any evidence of it around the grave. In addition, decades of moisture and mold had made the window all but opaque and impenetrable by even the brightest police-issue flashlight, which the boys had, of course, borrowed from Lowell's father. They found it much creepier not seeing Dr. Dumont, knowing that as they stared down into the glass-topped hole, an unseen skull grinned back at them from six feet below.

Lowell dropped himself heavily onto the flat stone, rapped on the window, and shouted at the top of his lungs, "Helloooooo, Dr. Dumont." He placed an apple on top of the window.

They could thank Moss and Feaster for this little tradition. The gravediggers wove quite a different tale about the grave of Dr. Dumont. According to them, Dr. Dumont was insane and could reanimate monsters from sewed-together corpse parts that he had robbed from the town cemetery—this town cemetery. He was eventually caught and hanged for his crimes, but the people of Cowlmouth were so terrified that he had unlocked the secrets of resurrection that they installed the window so that they could check on his corpse to ensure he was politely moldering the way God intended, instead of rising again to terrorize the town. Moss and Feaster advised Douglas that an apple a visit would help keep this mad doctor away. Lowell and Douglas found the idea funny enough to oblige it more often than not.

"That was a big funeral," said Douglas.

"Probably the biggest one Cowlmouth has seen in a long time." Lowell mispronounced the town's name on purpose, "Cowl-mouth" the way it looked, instead of "Cowl-muth," the way the founders had intended. Lowell wasn't from New England; he'd moved there from Maryland. Lowell had once told Douglas that the place where he was born crawled with water-blue crabs that turned bright red when you cooked them. You had to be careful where you stepped, or your toes would get scissored by the crab's giant, toothy claws. He had whipped off a shoe and shown Douglas scars on his foot as proof. Lowell moved to Cowlmouth with his father and younger brother sometime around the fourth grade, shortly after his mother's death. It took him a while to get into the habit of pronouncing the town name correctly. New England town names often follow their own rules of pronunciation. Then again, so did the entire state of Maryland.

"You'd be that popular, too, if you made awesome hot dogs." Lowell had changed from the shirt and pants he had been wearing for the funeral to a pair of jeans and a red flannel shirt that did nothing to dispel his scarecrow-ness. Douglas had surrendered his jacket, but still wore the lizard tie around his neck, pulled loose.

"Did your family get Mrs. Laurent's funeral?" Lowell asked.

"Yes."

"Did you go to it?"

"No, I had homework. But I watched Moss and Feaster bury her."

"Did you see her face?"

"No, they wouldn't let me."

Lowell nodded as if that made sense. "Oh, right. They told you she was a gorgon. Do you know how she died?"

"Do any of these questions have anything to do with your big news?"

"Keep your tie on, I'm getting there." Lowell reached into the back pocket of his jeans and pulled out a sweaty newspaper page that was folded almost to the point of being crumpled.

"Is your Internet broken?"

"Shut up. I promised you a genuine, real-life monster, and here it is. Take a look." A large, bold headline proclaimed itself through the newspaper creases:

MURDER IN COWLMOUTH

Lowell read it aloud for added emphasis, purposefully mispronouncing the name of the town again.

Douglas took the paper from his hands. "What? Murder? No way. That doesn't happen in Cowlmouth. The worst crime here is people forgetting to pay their parking meters."

"You're going to want to keep reading."

Douglas quickly sped through the rest of the column. "Wait. Mrs. Laurent was murdered?"

"Yeah. Like in a crime movie. Or a horror movie. Or a comedy movie. All movies have murders in them, I think."

"Who did it?"

"Nobody knows."

"And why would somebody murder that poor old woman? This doesn't make sense. There's hardly anything worth reading in this article."

"But there's more."

"More than murder?"

"She was marked." Lowell looked around to make sure the dead weren't listening too closely. "I overheard my dad talking to somebody on the phone in his office at the house. Through the vent in the hallway, you know?" That vent had gotten them both close to trouble too many times over the years. Lowell reached down and took a big bite out of Dr. Dumont's apple before replacing it on the glass. "Dad said that Mrs. Laurent had an M cut into her face."

"A what?"

"An M, as in letter of the alphabet. You're going to need to master all twenty-six before they let you pass sixth grade." Lowell roughly ground the grass under one of his heels into the grave dirt. "The M was carved right into her cheek."

"Into her cheek?"

"Yup. Like it was wet sidewalk cement."

Douglas listened for a few moments to a group of crows fiercely cawing to each other a few dozen plots away. "I didn't see that in the newspaper article."

"Newspapers never tell the whole story. See, the letter is a detail about Mrs. Laurent's murder that the police don't want the general public to know. That's why the newspapers aren't reporting it. It's *special evidence*." Lowell was almost beaming with this secret knowledge. "The M was a signature, the killer's mark. And you know what that means?"

Douglas stared down into the glass square of Dr. Dumont's grave. The creeps rising up his spine and down his arms had nothing to do with the naked skull at the bottom of the shaft. "No, what?"

"It means that this murder wasn't a random crime." Lowell's eyes grew wide. "My dad thinks that because the murderer marked Mrs. Laurent, he'll kill again. That's why the police need to keep some details of the crime secret. So that they can make sure they have the right guy when they catch him. Only the real killer will know those details. And you and me now, of course."

Douglas missed most of that explanation. In fact, he only caught two words, which he repeated weakly, "Kill again?"

"Yup."

Lowell seemed to be excited about the whole thing. He'd only been slightly more excited about the meat-balls. Big news. But *big* isn't how Douglas would have described it. *Troubling* was a good word. *Terrifying* was a better one. Certainly a thousand other words before *exciting*. But *monster* seemed right.

Douglas looked around. A strange feeling was bor-ing its way up into his throat from his stomach like something had hatched down there. His head swam and his ears seemed to pop with a sound like every tombstone in the cemetery had toppled and slammed to the ground. Suddenly, for the first time in his life, he didn't want to be in Cowlmouth Cemetery. He didn't want to be surrounded by dead people.

Death Douglas got.

Murder, that was different. Murder was a puzzle to be solved in stories. A word to be ignored on the boring newscasts his father liked to watch. *Murder* was an adult word. A coffee-drinker's word. The type archaically printed in newspapers. It didn't have a meaning in real life. Not in Douglas's real life, anyway. Not in Douglas's Cowlmouth.

"Low?"

"What?"

"Why an *M*?"

Lowell picked the apple up again, hooked his arm, and sent the fruit in a graceful arc deeper into the cemetery. "For murder, I guess. *M* for murder." The crows immediately attacked the missile when it hit the ground. "Or *M* for monster."

CHAPTER 5

The polished mahogany lid of the coffin slowly lowered, eclipsing the moon-white silk of the interior until a soft thud announced complete darkness inside. After Douglas had closed the coffin, he took a rag and a can of cleaner and began removing finger smudges from the long brass handles. Once they were shiny enough to glow, he attacked the thin skim of dust on the smooth wooden surfaces of the casket. His father was a couple of caskets away, pushing a broad-headed broom around the dark wood floor that bordered a pair of large red rugs.

The showroom was the second largest room in the house, behind the chapel. It had wide floor planks, dark beams in the ceiling, walls painted in pale cream, and an old granite fireplace that hadn't been used in decades, except by the squirrels that built nests in the chimney. It had originally been two rooms, but had been combined to accommodate as many caskets as the local fire code would allow them to display in the space.

The oblong boxes lined the walls and formed a grid in the center of the room. Each box was set on a thick, transparent stand that, when the light from the overhead fixtures threw the shadows of the caskets directly beneath them, made the boxes look like they were floating. The caskets ranged in style from simple to grand. Most were more box than a dead person would ever need, but, as his father was fond of saying of many aspects of their trade, "Not for the deceased."

Douglas took a deep breath and threw a question out among the caskets, one that he'd been keeping in check on a fraying leash inside since he and his father had started cleaning.

"Was Mrs. Laurent murdered?"

The broom in his father's hands froze. Mr. Mortimer studied the rounded end of the wooden handle as if it were suddenly the most important object in the universe. A lump at the upper corner of his jaw spasmed.

When he finally spoke, he seemed to be addressing the broom handle. "There are a thousand conversations I want to have with you, Douglas. This isn't really one of them."

"The news said that Mrs. Laurent was murdered." He was careful to leave Lowell's name out of it.

"Have I ever told you about the birds and the bees? Because I suddenly feel like having that talk."

"They both die."

"Right. *That* birds and the bees talk. We'll have to have the other one sometime." Douglas's father leaned the broom against the wall and started flipping through the pages of a thick leather binder on the fireplace mantel. It was a catalogue of special-order casket designs. Douglas sometimes liked to take the binder and lay down with it on the rug, flipping through the pages and memorizing the names of the brands and designs like they were the genuses and species of animals in a book of natural history. After a few seconds of page fluttering, Mr. Mortimer shut the book and looked up. "Listen, Douglas, murder is a lesson you honestly don't have to learn too much about right now. You're only eleven."

"I'm twelve. And I want to." Douglas moved to another open casket and peered inside. The velvet interior was almond-colored, triple-quilted, and the half-couch lid had an image of a willow tree embroidered on its underside. It looked much more inviting than the sagging wire-spring mattress upstairs in his room. He carefully closed the lid. They closed the caskets every evening. Even though everyone in the house was used to death, a casket lid accidentally banging shut was a generally unpleasant noise to hear in a funeral home in the dead of night. Plus, it could damage the expensive inventory.

Douglas's father walked over to the urn shelf, which took up almost an entire wall of the showroom and was loaded with about two dozen of the ash vases in a wide range of shapes and colors, like the treasures of some looted foreign tomb. He slowly ascended a small step-ladder, and plucked an elaborately detailed piece from the top shelf. Drawing a soft cloth from his pocket, he began cleaning the urn, which was emerald-colored, spider-webbed in gold filigree, and adorned with a small black-and-white picture of a young woman with curly dark hair and long eyelashes. This ash holder was the only urn on the display wall with actual cremated remains in it . . . those of Douglas's grandmother. Mr. Mortimer liked to think that having it here in the showroom kept his mother a part of the business. "Mom always wanted to be a model," he'd once told Douglas. Mr. Mortimer carefully put the urn back on the shelf and returned to floor level.

"I think there's a saying about putting genies back in bottles. I'll have to remember it when I explain this to your mother later." He looked uncertainly at Douglas across the casket lids. "We might as well go sit down for this." He led Douglas out of the showroom and toward the sitting room where they met with families about funeral arrangements.

The large house had been renovated, refurbished, and updated many times since Douglas's great-grand-father, Hammond Mortimer, turned the place into a funeral home sometime around the turn of the twentieth century. The only room that had remained almost untouched over those hundred years was the sitting room.

Paintings of famous funerals like Jesus Christ being laid in his tomb, the Norse god Balder sent out on his ship-born pyre, and Alexander the Great driving the funeral carriage of his general, Hephaestion, covered the walls. A small glass cabinet at the back of the room held six-inch-tall Mexican funerary figures—hollow clay effigies of beasts and people that were buried with the dead to keep them company in the afterlife. A pair of wooden African death masks adorned spaces on either side of the entrance, while on a table in the corner, a small bronze statue of the sarcophagus of the Egyptian boy-king Tutankhamun stood. The whole room was a history lesson in funeral custom and lore.

Douglas and his father sat down on one of the simple green couches facing each other across a low glass coffee table. For a few moments, they both stared at the vase of fresh plastic flowers and the fan of Mortimer Family Funeral Home pamphlets on the table.

"I don't know," his father began. "Your mother and I have been mercilessly up front with you about death. We've had to be." Mr. Mortimer waved a hand around in a small gesture that somehow encompassed the entire house and four generations of Mortimers. "You're probably better equipped to deal with death than most adults. I mean, I think so." He paused. "But murder . . ."

"So Mrs. Laurent was murdered?"

Mr. Mortimer nodded slowly. "In this business, we go out of our way to emphasize how much death is a part of life. How natural and, I don't know, right it is. And while, sure, that's a way to comfort the bereaved, it's also a way for us to cope with what we do, dealing with the dead day in and day out. But murder . . . I mean, technically, all deaths are natural. People die. Whether it's quietly in their sleep or in a horrible accident, it's just death when it all comes down to it. But murder . . . that's different. It's kind of like a death that shouldn't have happened. Or, I don't know. It's a terrible kind of death, and it makes us react with far worse than grief or sadness. Anger. Terror. Black emotions." Mr. Mortimer stared for a moment at a model of a terracotta warrior in the corner and blew out air from his cheeks. "I think I'm going about this the wrong way. What do you think about murder?"

Douglas carefully pushed aside the black stripes of hair on his forehead. "I don't know." In his head, the word conjured a vague, menacing image of a shadowy man with a bloody knife in a gloved hand. "Murder happens all the time, right? I mean, if the funeral home were in a big city, we'd have murder victims every day."

"Well, it doesn't happen all the time, even in cities. And here, yes, it's pretty rare." Mr. Mortimer looked at his son with more certainty. "Douglas, there's a lot of evil in the world. A lot of good, too, but a lot of evil. I've eaten, drank, breathed, and worn death my entire life. And I still find it unfathomable that one person can kill another, that the person on the table whose suit jacket I'm adjusting could be there because somebody else put him there on purpose. When it comes right down to it, murderers are broken people. Or bad people. Actually, not bad. Bad is when I caught you and Lowell sneaking out to the graveyard at night when you were nine. Evil. That's what they are. Evil. Monsters, really."

"Monsters," echoed Douglas.

"Yeah, monsters. I don't know. I think that's about as good an answer as I can give you. It's inadequate, and, well, the whole thing plain stinks, if I'm honest, both the fact of it and how difficult it is to explain."

"Who murdered Mrs. Laurent?"

"I don't know. Nobody does. But Lowell's dad is working on it, and you know what a good detective he is. Chief Pumphrey'll find out who did this evil thing, and the murderer will be punished and put somewhere he won't be a danger to anybody. That's the important thing. Until then, your mom and I want you to be extra careful. Don't go anywhere alone. Don't talk to strangers. Don't go out at night."

Douglas filled in the unspoken conclusion. *So you don't get murdered.*

"How did it happen?"

"Not important, Douglas. Well, I guess it is. No sense in me leaving holes in the story for your imagination to plug with all sorts of ghastly ideas worse that the, well, ghastly facts. Mrs. Laurent was out by herself at night. And she was killed. Stabbed." Mr. Mortimer winced. "Okay, that was probably one word of explanation too far. You understand, though?"

Douglas nodded and decided not to push it and ask about the M on Mrs. Laurent's cheek. Maybe he'd ask Eddie the next time he saw him.

"Have we ever had a funeral for a murder victim before?"

Mr. Mortimer pursed his lips and turned his head to look out the window. "I don't think so. At least, not while I've been here. But your great-grandfather did. A long time ago. At least, that's what he told me. It was supposed to have happened at a house over at the bottom of Chatman Street, near Druid Park. That place has been abandoned since I was a kid. Do you know about Death House? Do kids even still call it that?"

Douglas shook his head. It was an unfamiliar name to him.

"Anyway, they say something bad happened there. A man went crazy on his entire family . . ." He stopped and sighed. "I'm not sure, though. I could never quite tell if my grandfather was putting me on. He had a morbid sense of humor." Mr. Mortimer winked at Douglas. "My grandfather had a morbid sense of everything. He *was* a mortician, you know." Douglas's father reached out and straightened his son's tie. "So, are you okay?"

"I guess."

"You don't have to be." Mr. Mortimer looked up at the wide strip of crown molding that framed the ceiling. It had been carved to depict a New Orleans jazz funeral, a procession of musicians with brass instruments and dancers with parasols eternally parading above the room. "Tell you what. Why don't you go on up to your room, get ready for bed, and read for a bit. I'll finish the showroom and take care of the chapel by myself."

"Sure, Dad. Thanks." Douglas tried to sound as cheery as he could, as if everything was okay now and he would completely forget about it all by breakfast. But his relieved expression was as much a mask as the African ones on the wall or King Tut's golden faceplate. Truth was, what his father had told him had only made things worse.

Worse than murder.

Worse than murder in Cowlmouth.

Worse than a murder victim in the basement of his own house with an *M* carved in her cheek.

He'd never really thought about it before, but if death can be unnatural, then every word of comfort and consolation he'd ever heard was a lie. It was like being told your whole life how safe airplanes are and then seeing the wreckage of a crash scattered across a field on TV.

If some deaths were unnatural, maybe they all were. Maybe death wasn't any kind of completion, no finish line in a race, no last page in a book. Maybe death was just horrible no matter how it happened. Maybe the ritual that his family had dedicated itself to for generations was a fraud. Maybe it was a way of hiding the awfulness that was the end of life, or even the awfulness of life, itself.

Douglas didn't read in bed as his father had suggested. He just lay there, cringing every time one of those thoughts crossed his mind.

When he finally did fall asleep, the boy who had slept in a bedroom above the dead for his entire life had his first nightmare.

SEPTEMBER 16

FRIDAY

CHAPTER 6

Douglas chewed on the pink eraser of a No. 2 pencil and stared back into the hollow triangular eyes that were leering into his soul.

Miss Farwell had jumped the gun again in decorating her classroom for the upcoming holiday. Last year, her Easter decorations had gone up before the March snow had melted. Her St. Patrick's Day had collided with her St. Valentine's Day in a magnificent holy war. She'd even put up Christmas decorations before they'd gotten to Thanksgiving break. The territorial fights between the reindeer and the turkeys were savage.

This year, her Back to School decorations hardly had time to greet the returning students before being retired for the year. The card-stock rulers and books and globes that adorned the walls, the poster on the bulletin board of the shiny apple with a protruding worm in a graduation cap and glasses, the long Welcome Back banner that ran almost the width of the chalkboard with words spelled out in pencils—they'd all been replaced before September was barely halfway over.

Now, the sixth-grade classroom was a darker world. Chains of black construction paper bats hung in loops from the ceiling tiles. Fake spiderwebs stretched along the edges of the bookshelves. Paper ghosts, mummies, vampires, and werewolves danced across the beige cement-block walls. Miss Farwell had covered the back of the students' chairs with large paper gravestones bearing their names under the letters RIP. She'd put a four-foot-tall inflatable Frankenstein's monster in the back corner of the classroom. Her bulletin board was festooned with flyers for this year's Cowlmouth Fall Carnival. And, of course, there was the orange plastic jack-o'-lantern with its glowing light bulb brain that sat on the corner of her desk, staring straight at Douglas in his unfortunate front row seat.

In six weeks, it would be Halloween. In six weeks,

everybody would be as okay with death as Douglas Mortimer was.

Except that Douglas wasn't really okay with death anymore. Not since he learned a week ago that murder wasn't just a video game plot point, that it wasn't always the natural end that he'd thought it to be, and that, maybe, it never had been.

Murder scared him, of course. It was something that made you think twice before staying out too late and hurry past dark alleyways. It was one of the reasons every child was told never to talk to strangers.

But, more than being scared of it, murder bothered Douglas.

He looked down at the test on his desk. He had finished it a good five minutes ago. All except for one question, a fill-in-the-blank:

Good is to Evil as Clean is to _____.

Douglas knew that the answer Miss Farwell was looking for was "dirty." But that's not the answer that made sense to him.

Good. Evil. The words, themselves, seemed to tell their own tales. *Good* looked insufficient, monosyllabic, almost goofy, and very round like Reverend Ahlgrim. *Evil* was all pointy, strong and deadly looking, and somehow, with its long *E*, pleasant to say.

He didn't like it one bit.

M for murder. *M* for monster. Douglas couldn't even sign the test without the large *M* of his last name standing out to him in ominous strokes. It was as if the letter had been cut into his own brain instead of Mrs. Laurent's cheek.

With effort, he tried to ignore both the heavy thoughts weighing on him and the scrutiny of the jack-o'-lantern as he halfheartedly filled in the answer to the question. When he put his pencil down to wait for Miss Farwell to call time, he saw something strange out of the corner of his eye. The view outside the classroom door window was usually of the large bank of red lockers across the hallway, but now, a small, round, furry head with big black eyes and two tall brown horns like a bull's horns slowly rose past the bottom edge. It stopped, glanced back and forth, and slowly slid along the pane before disappearing past the side of glass. It then reversed course, moving back across the lower part of the window before disappearing again.

Douglas almost had to stick his pencil back in his mouth to stifle a laugh. A few echoed titters around the room told him he wasn't the only one who'd seen the joke, but he was probably the only one to recognize its source. The furry head came into view again, confirming his suspicions when a third eye, this one small and clear and blue popped up under the hair . . . and widened in terror as the door opened.

"Mr. Pumphrey, what are you doing?" Miss Farwell looked down at Lowell, a stern expression on her face, the one she'd patented sometime in the last few years and only rarely meant.

Lowell, on his knees, a pair of sunglasses pushed up in his yellow stack of hair and a pair of plastic horns planted on his head, missed only enough of a beat to stammer out an "Uh . . ." before explaining, "I dropped my books." He gestured around where, surprisingly, there were indeed books and papers scattered around him.

Her eyes narrowed in suspicion. "I see. Nice horns."

"Thanks. Family heirloom." He took them off to give her a better view of the two pieces of plastic connected by a black arc of headband. When she ignored it, he popped them right back onto his temples.

"Well, hurry and pick up your things. The last bell will ring soon, and it's Friday, so I can't make any promises about controlling the sixth-grade stampede."

"Yes, ma'am." Before the door fully closed, Lowell was able to squeeze in a quick monster face at Douglas.

Minutes later, the tests collected, the homework assigned, and every student's bottom shifting on the edge of his or her seat like rodeo cowboys behind a gate, the bell signaling the end of the school day clanged out its metal cry of freedom. A glorious cacophony of books being slammed shut and paper being crumpled and supplies being gathered and crammed haphazardly into backpacks filled the room. It was a happy hullabaloo.

Douglas slipped out the classroom door to find Lowell waiting.

"I didn't hear you drop your books."

"Ha. I didn't. Spread them around real quiet-like to give myself an alibi in case your teacher saw me. Funny, though, right?"

"Yeah, good one." Nobody is better at faking alibis than a police officer's son.

The duo held their own in the torrent of students pouring down the school hallway and through the heavy doors at the front of the building. Outside, the bright sky was taking on the slightest tinge of twilight, warning of the much shorter days to come. They walked across the central lawn, and past the school building where Lowell spent his time when he wasn't playing around outside of sixth-grade classroom doors.

As they meandered toward the parking lot, a sudden dark spot cropped up in Douglas's vision. One blink later, the spot resolved itself into a short, pale girl with long dark hair and a purple stone on her finger. She waved as she passed. Lowell nodded a silent greeting but kept walking.

"Who was that?" Douglas asked without really meaning to.

"Audrey. Interested?"

"Shut up. Just curious. I saw her at Mr. Stauffer's funeral."

"Yeah, she's in my class. Her father's an ambulance driver or something." Lowell slowed his pace and squinted an eye at Douglas. "You were in the same school building with her last year. Like me." A large grin slowly broke out on his face. "Uh-oh. Sounds like somebody's radar got recalibrated over the summer."

"Again, shut up."

"It's okay, man. The Fall Carnival's coming up soon, you know." He pointed to a series of posters tacked to a wall of the school. One said GATHER YOUR FAMILY FOR A FUN PHOTO AT THE COWLMOUTH FALL CARNIVAL. COSTUMES PROVIDED. A picture on it showed a family of five all made up to look like characters from *Alice in Wonderland*. Another had an image of Godzilla holding a pumpkin above his head. The poster read COWLMOUTH FALL CARNIVAL MONSTER PUMPKIN CONTEST. $5,000 IN PRIZES. "You could ask her to go with you. Say the word, and I'll introduce you."

"I've got a few words. Real nasty ones. All for you."

"You're definitely going to the Fall Carnival, though, right?"

Cowlmouth was a nice place, but Cowlmouth during the Cowlmouth Fall Carnival was perfection. During the festival, it was as if every business and house and park and citizen shifted slightly in time and space to fit together exactly as they were meant to. The carnival had been tradition since the town's founding. Cowlmouth could have been the birthplace of two astronauts, four movie stars, and Wi-Fi, and its welcome sign would still have read HOME OF THE COWLMOUTH FALL CARNIVAL.

"Of course."

"What're you up to tomorrow afternoon? Cemetery?"

"No. Mom wants help with some errands—groceries, funeral business at the church, nothing exciting. I doubt my folks will let me out after that. They're being real protective, what with Mrs. Laurent and all."

Lowell's eyes brightened and the horns that were for some reason still on his head seemed to perk up. "The monster."

Douglas grabbed Lowell by the arm and stopped walking. He looked around to make sure nobody was within earshot and then lowered his voice. "Has your dad found out anything new?"

"Nope. Not that I know of, anyway. I've listened at the vent every night this week, but nothing." If Chief Pumphrey ever found out that his son was eavesdropping on his work conversations, no alibi would save him.

"Maybe that's good news. I almost don't want the murderer caught. I wish he'd just vanish forever."

"Oh, Dad'll catch him. He just needs the killer to strike again."

"What?" Douglas grimaced at his friend.

"Simple math, man. Two murders are twice the evidence, twice the chance the monster might make a mistake . . ."

"Twice the murder victims. That's a rotten thing to say."

"A murderer is on the loose. The whole situation is rotten."

"What if he's already left Cowlmouth?"

"Then some other town's Mrs. Laurent will be killed. And, again, he'll be easier to find. Every body's a clue." Lowell widened his eyes and waggled his fingers at Douglas.

They continued to the school parking lot. Sticking out from all the minivans, SUVs, and compact cars was a sleek, long, black hearse taking up two spaces.

"Looks like your ride's here, Doug."

SEPTEMBER 17

SATURDAY

CHAPTER 7

If there was one place where the word *death* was spoken more times than at a funeral home, it was at church. The word was never more than a grave's width away from the topic of every sermon, and everybody who attended seemed to be okay with it being constantly brought up. As a result, Douglas usually felt more or less at home in the sanctuary, even when the church was empty except for himself, his mother, and Reverend Ahlgrim. Today Reverend Ahlgrim had a large black Bible clutched in his right hand and a four-foot-long bright green rubber snake coiled around his left shoulder like a rope.

"No tie today, Douglas?" asked the reverend.

They were standing below the pulpit, in the same

spot where Mr. Stauffer's coffin had been a week ago, and countless more before his. Douglas often thought of it as the dead spot of the church. Looming above them was the stained glass eye, blind now with nobody at the pulpit, and softly glowing in the artificial light installed behind the panes.

Mrs. Mortimer tousled Douglas's hair. "Every once in a while, I can convince him to let his neck breathe." Douglas's mother was tall, taller than his father and Reverend Ahlgrim at least, with thick red hair, a fine spray of freckles on her face, and a fondness for gold jewelry. The hand that had messed up Douglas's hair had no less than four rings on it and her own neck was being strangled by three different lengths of chain, the middle one bearing a delicate casket-shaped charm with her initials on it.

"So how's school? You're in sixth grade now, right?" Without pausing for an answer to either question, Reverend Ahlgrim continued, "Would you believe me if I told you that someday, when you're older, you're going to miss being in school?"

Douglas smoothed his hair and shook his head, not wanting to risk the eternal penalty for calling a clergy-man a liar.

"Oh, well. You will." Reverend Ahlgrim turned to Mrs. Mortimer. "What can I do for you today?"

"Just dropping by to touch base. I think you're supposed to be conducting a service next week at our chapel. Oh, and I wanted to thank you again for conducting Mrs. Laurent's service at such short notice. On top of everything else out of the ordinary with that funeral, of course her pastor would have been recovering from heart surgery." Mrs. Mortimer pulled her smartphone out of her purse and called up her calendar with a few taps of a blood-red fingernail.

"Poor Mrs. Laurent," the reverend said, casting his eyes down into the church's dead spot and grabbing at the snake around his shoulder like it was a loose suspender. "I keep thinking about that funeral . . ." Reverend Ahlgrim looked down at Douglas as if he were suddenly reminded that he was there. "But I'm being too morbid for a sixth-grade boy."

"It's okay. His father had a 'talk' with him about the whole thing." She rolled her eyes. "Besides, Douglas is good at death." She tousled his hair again, and he winced, although not because he was going to have to fix his hair.

"I'm sorry. Sometimes I lose all sense of propriety

when I talk," said Reverend Ahlgrim. "Especially when it comes to death. I teach children in Sunday School about Cain killing Abel, Moses murdering the Egyptian, Elijah summoning bears to kill children for making fun of him. You get a little used to it. Sometimes, I think death is more my business than yours, Mrs. Mortimer."

Douglas nodded in agreement, even though neither his mother nor the preacher were looking at him.

"What's your schedule like this month?" asked Mrs. Mortimer.

"I'm not sure. If it's not Sunday, I don't know what day it is or what's going on. Let me get my planner from my office. Hey, Douglas, check this out. I picked it up today from the toy store for one of the Sunday School classes." He pulled the scaly coil off his shoulder and dangled the long, springy piece of green fork-tongued rubber in front of him. "They're doing Adam and Eve."

Douglas looked at his mom, who somehow communicated without even quivering an eyelash that he should accept the gesture.

"Cool," he said, taking the snake and the opportunity to escape from the conversation. He wandered toward the back of the church toward the giant Jesus on the wall.

Douglas had hung out under many Jesi in his day, waiting while his parents conducted business in holy places. He'd seen the splayed savior in all sizes, positions, and styles: looking down in death, up in supplication, straight out in accusation. He'd seen plain wooden figures with vaguely carved features, Jesus-less crosses like lowercase *Ts*, and surreal icons made out of wire and metal that only kind of looked like a person on a cross. The one at the back of Cowlmouth Center Church—the same one under which he had stood while handing out programs for Mr. Stauffer's funeral—was enormous, dark, carved out of oak, and highly polished. This Jesus looked up at the ribbed ceiling of the church. Black rivulets ran from his eyes, chest, hands, and feet. On a wooden scroll at the foot of the cross were the words, *Eloi, Eloi, Lama Sabachthani.* It looked to Douglas like something a magician might incant before making an assistant disappear.

Douglas settled himself beneath the cross with his back to the wall. He dropped the snake in a loose pile beside him, promptly pulling his phone out of his pocket. He was on the first level of a game that involved a zookeeper trying to corral escaped animals. The game started easy enough with turtles and hedgehogs, but eventually you had to herd wily monkeys, flying eagles, and dangerous tigers back into their cages.

Before he could even get his first turtle into its tank, a thought struck him that made him crane his neck and look up at the cross. Jesus was being murdered. He could almost see the *M* forming in the creases of Jesus's wooden cheek.

Douglas had always known that these statues depicting a dying or dead man. Heck, it was another reason he felt at home in church. Back at the funeral home, if there was ever a day where there wasn't a corpse somewhere on the premises, the house felt empty and odd.

He also knew the story of Jesus. That happens when you attend as many funeral services as he had. Jesus died and rose from the dead. People like to think about that when their loved ones die. But now that he looked at the story from a different angle, the comfort seemed to drain completely out from it. The dead Christ no longer seemed like a symbol of hopeful resurrection, but of a world full of violence.

What affected him more than the story, though, was that they blatantly displayed a murder victim on the church wall. On almost every church wall in town, in fact. Why would they do that? He was trying to figure out a way to not think about murder, while churches tried to remind their members of it every Sunday. It baffled him. And it terrified him for another reason.

Murder was everywhere. Even the safest places.

Before he could go much further with the thought, he heard the familiar chime of his mother's cell phone, and then a hurried exchange involving her, whoever was on the other end, and Reverend Ahlgrim.

Suddenly, Mrs. Mortimer was barreling down the aisle, sweeping Douglas up by his hand, and rushing him out to the car. The snake lay where he had dropped it, evil-looking and venomous on the red carpet. Douglas neither protested nor asked questions. He had heard two words in the flurry of conversation at the front of the church:

"Another murder."

SEPTEMBER 20

TUESDAY

CHAPTER 8

Under the glowing blanket tent of his bed, Douglas held a worn paperback copy of *Something Wicked This Way Comes*. He was illuminating the text with a flashlight nestled between his shoulder and neck. On the cover was an illustration of a long, black train belching giant nightmare shapes from its smokestack into a moonlit sky. But he wasn't so much reading the book as staring into its pages, churning over what had happened three days ago and worrying what was about to happen tonight as a result.

Eventually, he gave up, tossing back the blanket and throwing the book onto his bedside table. The alarm clock that the book landed on said it was three minutes past midnight.

Other than it being strangely neat, Douglas's room had many of the normal features of a twelve-year-old's room. On his desk was a pile of worn comic books. In another corner, a basket of dirty clothes took up a defensive posture. A glow-in-the-dark topographical map of the moon covered almost the entire wall above his bed. However, there were a few objects that would have been out of place in the rooms of most twelve-year-olds. Like Douglas's collection of funeral programs, each one bearing the image of a dead person and balancing out the pile of comic books on his desk. A jar of grave dirt sat on a shelf, a present from his grandfather that had been collected from a famous cemetery in London. Strung across the ceiling was a garland of one-sided cardboard tombstones, a repurposed Halloween decoration that happened to fit the season, but which was really a perennial accent. And then there were the flowers. Douglas had more flowers in his room than a hospital patient. But all of his blossoms, blooms, and buds were plastic. Each bit of fake flora had been collected from a funeral service or a grave site. To Douglas, they were just another part of the business of life at a funeral home, as distant from wildflowers as gravestones were from actual stones.

Douglas pivoted out of bed and crept silently over to one of his windows, which looked out over the small visitor parking lot beside the house. He could see the family hearse and also the black van they used for removals when the dead didn't need to ride in style. Christopher's rust-red Grand Am, which was older than Douglas, was parked in the lot, too, along with Eddie's small, green Civic. The four vehicles looked to Douglas like horses asleep in their stalls. Three of the vehicles were parked there almost every night. If Eddie's was there, that meant he was pulling a late night, which also meant that Douglas would be pulling an even later one.

When Douglas and his mother had arrived home after meeting with Reverend Ahlgrim, they had found an ominous funeral procession of cars crammed chaotically in the parking lot and against the granite curb in front of the house. Douglas recognized Chief Pumphrey's dark blue patrol car easily among the rest of the police cars. The chief's had a small, fuzzy black bear wearing a tiny police cap dangling from the rearview mirror. There was also a large white van with orange lights on its roof and the words MEDICAL EXAMINER painted along the side in large black letters.

Douglas had seen that vehicle one other time in his life, a week and a half ago, when Mrs. Laurent had been delivered to the funeral home. At the time, he'd asked his father about it out of innocent curiosity. Turns out, the van was an official police vehicle, and the "Medical Examiner" title referred to Dr. Coffman. Apparently, he didn't only make you say *Ahhhh* and hand out lemon candy.

Douglas's mother had made him go around back and up the stairs to the residence on the second story, while she went through the front door of the funeral home. He'd obeyed more out of confusion than anything else. As he went around back, he passed Christopher, who was leaning against the side of the green-paneled house, breathing heavily like he'd run a couple miles. Douglas tried to speak with him, but Christopher only shook his head and waved dismissively.

Once in his own room, Douglas started to regret not pushing the issue. Unlike Lowell, Douglas didn't have a vent that he could use as an oracle. He could have sat on the top of the stairs, but with so many people down below, it would be difficult to make out anything coherent, and there was a real chance someone would have caught him eavesdropping. As it was, from the front door of his room, only a buzz of low conversation wafted up to him.

It almost didn't matter, though. Douglas could guess most of what was going on down there. They'd found another victim. And that victim had an M carved into his or her cheek. The officials had brought the body to the funeral home to use the morgue facilities.

Three days later, he was still highly aware of the murder victim two floors below. He had slowly realized, with a gradually sickening feeling that burned the tissue of his stomach, that he had to see it—he had to see the M.

As he gazed out into the hazy dimness of the town, he heard the back door swing quietly open and saw the short form of Eddie Brunswick cross the parking lot. Eddie opened the door of the Civic, started the engine after a few seconds of fiddling, and drove off down the road.

It was time.

Douglas punched a random letter four times into his phone, and hit SEND. He would delete the short string of characters later, but if his parents somehow ever discovered them, it would look like an accidental text message.

Douglas and Lowell had learned long ago that sneaking was only a minor sin, quickly forgiven. As a result, they had taken full advantage of the moral loophole on numerous occasions, although mostly just to visit the cemetery at night or to raid the refrigerator when they stayed over at each other's houses. Other than one midnight incident a couple of years before, when Douglas's father had been roused by a removal call, Douglas and Lowell had a perfect record of not being caught. Sometimes, Douglas would even slip downstairs late at night to watch the television in his father's office, but he'd never snuck down to the morgue. Certainly not by himself.

A lifetime of sneaking had taught Douglas to avoid walking down the middle of the hallway where the floorboards sagged slightly and could creak loud alarms into the nighttime silence. He knew to skip both the third and tenth steps for the same reason. He could, without barking a shin or bruising a forehead, navigate the whole house and funeral home in the dark. He didn't even use his flashlight, although he did bring it. It was heavy and silver and oddly comforting, even with the light off.

The morgue was in the basement. To get there, Douglas had to go downstairs and cross the showroom, the chapel, and a back storage room.

He passed by the living room on his way to the stairs. "Living rooms are important rooms in anybody's house," his grandfather had told him a long time ago, "but they are particularly important when your home is a mortuary."

Finally, Douglas made it to the head of the stairs and silently descended into the funeral home part of the house.

Normally, walking through a mortuary at night wouldn't have been too much of a problem for a boy that considered it home, but tonight as he glided through the maze of oblong boxes in the showroom, Douglas couldn't help imagining them filled with murder victims, each bearing a livid, bleeding M carved into their faces. One creak of a coffin lid would have sent him screaming for the stairs, near-perfect sneaking record or not. The chapel gave him barely more comfort as he passed the spot where Mrs. Laurent had lain in her closed casket just two weeks before.

He was extra careful crossing the chapel, as Christopher's room was above that space. Of course, Douglas was pretty sure that even had he pushed over one of the chapel benches and dragged it across the room, Christopher would barely stir, since sometimes Douglas's father had to bang for a long time on Christopher's door to wake him up for a late-night removal call.

Douglas went through the small back storeroom to a white door with large, black, metal letters tacked to it: Morgue. Douglas placed his hand on the handle and pulled. The door opened silently. His father made it a point to have Christopher regularly oil all the hinges in the entire place. Eerie creaks were not something a funeral home wanted its customers subjected to. Below Douglas, concrete steps descended into blackness.

He turned on his flashlight and walked gingerly downstairs. Sometimes, his father called this space the preparation room, but Eddie hated the softened terminology of the modern mortuary business. To Eddie, Douglas's father was an undertaker, not a funeral director; he prepared the bodies of corpses, not decedents; and don't get him started on the phrase *memory portrait*.

Even though Douglas's parents had been completely open about death, the morgue was still one place Douglas wasn't allowed free reign. Occasionally, he'd visit Eddie down there, but Eddie's job involved him doing things to the dead bodies that Douglas's parents didn't want him exposed to yet. Of course, had they known half the things that Eddie had shown Douglas down there, the Mortimer Family Funeral Home might have suddenly been in the market for both a new embalmer *and* a new heir.

Douglas shined his flashlight around the room. Eddie needed the best lighting to do his job, so Douglas didn't dare turn any on for fear that someone might notice the ultra-bright florescent glow through the small basement windows. Most of the surfaces that the beam bounced off were glass and stainless steel. A pair of horizontal human-sized metal tables with ceramic tops, gutters, and embalming stations dominated the room. Against the walls were various locked cabinets of chemical jars in a variety of colors and sleek-looking shiny implements that made you want to pick them up and twist them to catch the light. Tonight, everything seemed monochrome, like this was the laboratory of a mad scientist from an old monster movie. In truth, it was close enough to that. Here, Eddie made the dead live for one more day, a temporary resurrection to bring closure for family and friends, before his work was buried forever under dirt. Eddie's art was a humble one.

As Douglas continued to shine the flashlight aimlessly about the room, it caught a glint of crystal at one of the embalming stations—an etched tumbler filled with a thick, dark, purple liquid that smell faintly sweet and extremely strong. Eddie would have been mortified to know he'd left it out, so Douglas poured it down a nearby sink, rinsed it out, and stuck it in an unlocked cabinet. Eddie would never even know that he'd left it out.

Suddenly, a regular pattern of soft scratching noises stopped him cold. It was coming from the outside door, the one leading to the parking lot. Douglas heard it again, louder this time, and he started, almost upsetting a glass beaker near the sink. He swallowed his heart back into the appropriate spot in his chest and walked over to the door.

There were a lot of dangerous chemicals and valuable equipment in a funeral home, so the house had a security system. Douglas keyed in the code to temporarily deactivate it and opened the door.

"Anybody alive in here?"

For two seconds, Lowell was his usual self, eyes full of mischief and mouth full of merriment. As soon as he crossed the threshold of the morgue, his fire hissed wetly into steam.

"I don't think I could ever sleep in a house with a room like this."

"You've slept over here tons of times," Douglas reminded him, shutting the door and re-keying the security code.

"Good point." Lowell turned on his own flashlight, a black, sturdy police-issue piece of equipment that his father had given him on a past birthday. "Still, I don't think I could do it every night, all alone in my room, like you do. You should really talk your parents into getting you a sibling. Heck, a half dozen of them. I wonder how many times you guys have been outnumbered by corpses here."

"They're not the worst company. They mostly keep to themselves. I don't have to share anything with them. They let me watch whatever I want on TV."

"I've always liked you because you're weird. But, man. You. Are. Weird."

"We're putting this off, huh?"

"Yup."

"We don't have to do this."

"Like hockey sticks, we don't. We've got to see this."

"Yeah, we do. I guess. Actually, I'm not as sure as I was."

"Oh, you're sure. You know as well as I do why we've got to see the M. Somehow, it's worse not seeing it. At least I haven't had to live above it for three days."

Lowell was right, and that was exactly why the first thing Douglas had done upon arriving home that day, was to text Lowell to let him know what had happened. Douglas knew immediately that he would need to sneak into the morgue, but he also needed Lowell to be the one to suggest it first.

The three days had been rough for Douglas, especially with his parents giving him limited information, even after the sitting room talk with his father. Dr. Coffman had come to examine the body. Chief Pumphrey had come to examine the body. His father told him it was part of the autopsy process. Once that had been completed, it was in Eddie's hands to get the body ready for the funeral, which would be held tomorrow in the chapel. Tonight was their last chance to see the M before it disappeared under six feet of dirt and worms. Douglas was glad he didn't have to do it alone.

"Let's get this over with so that we can get on to the nightmares afterward." As Lowell spoke, his eyes skittered nervously across the morgue tables as if he expected to see the body there, chest cut open and eyes staring.

"It's in one of the refrigerator cabinets," said Douglas, pointing with his flashlight beam. One entire wall was made up of a morgue refrigerator, although it wasn't the type of refrigerator one would want to raid in the middle of the night, even though that's exactly what the two boys were there to do. The stainless steel refrigerator had nine square panels in three rows, like an empty tic-tac-toe board, each of which pulled out into a human-sized drawer. Nine was more than adequate for the needs of the Mortimer Family Funeral Home. As far back as Douglas could remember, the closest they had come to filling up all nine spaces at the same time was the night of a bad automobile accident. Douglas's father had given Eddie an extra two weeks of vacation not long after.

Lowell followed the beam of light with his eyes, but didn't move . . . his feet, at least. His head and neck were convulsing in quick jerks, signaling that Douglas should take the lead.

Douglas walked warily over to the cabinets. He'd opened drawers full of the deceased before. It wasn't a big deal. Except that this time it wasn't just a dead person—it was a murder victim. And that changed everything. He took a deep breath and chose the center drawer. The long shelf rumbled out with the obscenely mundane sound of metal tracks in metal grooves.

Douglas wasn't too concerned about the noise. The morgue was well isolated from the rest of the house, and he'd stood near its upstairs door many times without hearing a single clatter from Eddie below.

The drawer was empty.

Douglas exhaled and tried the next drawer. Empty, as well.

"Man, I really don't like this game," Lowell muttered behind him.

Douglas chose the left bottom drawer next.

"You're kidding me," was Lowell's response to its contents.

The drawer wasn't empty, but it didn't contain a corpse, either. Instead, the long shelf held a thick red sleeping bag, a pillow, and a plush gorilla in a brown coat and Sherlock Holmes hat.

"I've always thought that Eddie spent the night down here sometimes," Douglas remarked. "I guess it didn't occur to me to wonder where."

"And what does it mean that the gorilla is the least weird thing about this?" Lowell quipped.

Finally, after closing Eddie's impromptu bed, Douglas chose the center bottom drawer. It slid open to reveal a sheet-covered form, as white and pristine as the end of laundry day. He heard Lowell suck air through his teeth. Douglas, holding his flashlight in one hand, reached with his other to the head of the cadaver and quickly pulled the sheet down about a foot before yanking his hand away like he'd touched something slimy.

"It's possible that my eyes are closed in horror. What do you see, Doug?"

"A dead man."

Lowell shouldered up beside Douglas and took a look. Bright circles from two flashlights hovered over the pale face on the slab. "That . . . looks like a high schooler."

The young man on the slab had a dark, tangled mess of hair that Eddie had yet to arrange, a somewhat flat nose, and eyelashes that seemed too long on his widely spaced eyes, which were, thankfully, closed. "You know what's weird?" asked Douglas.

"Two boys sneaking into a morgue to see a dead body and not running away scared when they do?"

"There's no mark on his face. No M for murder." At Douglas's simple observation, Lowell leaned in closer. Both of the dead guy's cheeks were smooth, pale, and unblemished.

"Maybe you got two new clients today."

"Maybe. Easy enough to find out." Douglas replaced the sheet and pushed the body back into the dark and cold of the morgue refrigerator before trying the rest of the cabinets. He had to use Eddie's stepladder to reach the upper three. They all came up empty. There were no other bodies, only the one in the lower center cabinet. The one without an M on his cheek.

"Maybe you were wrong about all the commotion on Saturday."

"No. There was another murder."

"Maybe they were wrong. Or maybe this guy was murdered. Just not by a killer who signs his handiwork. That would be crazy. Cowlmouth suddenly full of murderers. We can check online tomorrow. See what the news says."

"We can check right now."

"The news?"

"No."

"What do you mean?"

"A real quick check. For wounds."

"Man, the admission price tonight was not supposed to include a full body search on a corpse. Only a quick peek and a terrified scream, followed by a brisk run back to the safety of my dinosaur sheets."

Douglas ignored his friend and opened the lower center cabinet again, sliding the white-sheeted form out slowly, so that the metal rails emitted only a soft rumble. Douglas pulled the sheet down past the cadaver's chin and stopped.

"Wait a minute." He bent closer. "Hold on." Douglas walked over to a small drawer on the far side of the room and returned with a scalpel. It was tiny, sharp, and didn't at all look right in a boy's hand. Lowell moved out of his way to the far side of the drawer so that it separated them like a sideways ping-pong table.

"What . . . are . . . you . . . doing?"

"Eddie calls this his tenth finger." Douglas lifted the scalpel in a trembling hand to the right cheek of the man. Pausing to get more control over the wavering piece of surgical steel, he carefully scraped away at the flesh.

"Aw, man. Don't touch it. Don't touch it. Aw, man." Lowell took a few steps back from the body.

"He has mortician's wax on his cheek. Eddie uses it to cover up facial scars for viewings."

"Oh." Suddenly Lowell's interest returned and he moved closer. "They're definitely going to know that we snuck down here now."

95

"I think I can reapply it. I've seen Eddie do it a few times. The wax is in one of the locked cabinets, but I know where he hides a key." By then, Douglas had removed enough of the wax to reveal what was underneath it. "Uh-oh."

Lowell let out a low whistle. "*S* does not stand for murder."

Once enough of the wax had been scraped away, there was no mistaking the sinuous letter that had been cut into the face of the man by his killer and stitched together by his embalmer.

"What do you think this means, Low? It's not a different killer, is it?"

"I don't think so, but what do I know? Maybe it's the same killer, and he's spelling something."

"I don't know too many words that start with *ms*."

"Maybe we haven't found the other letters. Or maybe the killer's dyslexic."

"Yeah." Douglas said, but he barely registered his friend's words. Something else had caught his attention, which was saying a lot since Douglas was standing over a dead body. The windows in the basement room were small, set close to the ceiling. Outside, the horizontal panes of glass were at ground level. There wasn't much to see through them at that moment—just night and grass that needed mowing. But Douglas thought he saw some of that night shift faintly, some of that grass move slightly. As he stared, he slowly moved the flashlight in an underhand arc across the floor and up the wall. Right before the circle of light hit the window, a flurry of motion outside made him call out loud enough that it almost penetrated the two floors to his parents' bedroom on the opposite side of the house.

"What's the matter?" Lowell turned around fast. "Did you see something?"

It took Douglas a few seconds to work up the saliva to answer. "Yes, outside the window. I saw something move outside the window."

Lowell stared at the small, black rectangle. Nothing stirred.

"Think it was Eddie?"

"I don't know."

"Let's give this guy his cheek back, and get the hockey sticks out of here."

SEPTEMBER 21

WEDNESDAY

CHAPTER 9

Douglas had never met him while he was alive. Now, in death, he had seen him three times in less than twenty-four hours. In the morgue last night, in the nightmares that followed, and now in the chapel for the funeral service. He'd only found out his name by glancing at a program: Marvin Brinsfield. Marvin, the murder victim.

The Mortimer Family Funeral Home chapel was officially called the Hammond Mortimer Memorial Chapel. It took up the part of the house that had once been a detached carriage house and was purposefully a simple affair. Plain wooden benches with blue cushions, a thin metal lectern at the front, and tall windows that arched at the top. All easily customizable to suit whichever religious rites needed to be suited.

It was six o'clock in the evening and the funeral wasn't scheduled to start for another hour, but Douglas had to pay his respects to the dead early. Soon, he would have to leave the coffin-side contemplation to the actual mourners. Marvin was currently reposed in front of the lectern in a cedar coffin with a soft red interior. His hair had been combed since Douglas had last seen him, and the layer of mortician's wax on his cheek somehow looked even better in the soft light of the chapel than when he had applied it by flashlight in the dark morgue the night before.

Of course, as Douglas stood again above the prostrate form of the murder victim, he wasn't so much paying his respects as he was thinking of the ragged *S* currently hidden on the deceased's cheek. Douglas had been thinking about it all day at school, and that inevitably made him think of the dark figure at the window. It seemed that his mind only went to bad places these days.

Beside him, a hand reached out and rested on the edge of the coffin as a smell of leather and formaldehyde entered his nostrils. The hand had a thick coat of hair on its back and knuckles, and its middle finger ended abruptly in a smooth nub at the first knuckle.

"Hi, Eddie."

"Nice tie." It was red with golden rectangles and sort of clashed with his gold and green name tag.

"Thanks."

"Good work, right? It's harder to make up young people. Older folks, they can look fine dead. Most of them look dead when they're alive, anyway. Younger ones, it's harder to do."

"Yeah, he looks good. You always do great work."

"Thanks. Although," Eddie paused for a few seconds, "I don't always have to do that work twice, you know."

A chill ran down Douglas's body, as if he'd been suddenly pushed into the morgue refrigerator downstairs. His stare remained on the cheek of the murdered man. "What do you mean?"

"I mean, I came in this morning to finish up Marvin, here, and discovered that somebody had undone some of my carefully crafted facial work and then reapplied their own."

For a few seconds, Douglas thought about trying to keep up the charade. "How'd you know it was me?" he finally asked.

"Because you did a pretty good job. Plus, you're the only one it could have been. I briefly, briefly thought that maybe the police wanted another look at the scar and your father had accommodated them. Heck, it wouldn't have surprised me with all the confusion that went on with Mrs. Laurent's corpse. But your father would have asked me to cover it again, not tried to do it himself."

"Sorry. We had to see the letter."

"We. The police chief's boy, right?"

"Yeah."

"So I guess that's how you knew about the letters in the first place. A friend in the know. Heck, you probably know more about the murders than I do."

"Not really. Low apparently knows just enough to get me in trouble."

"Ha. It's good to have a friend like that. Just don't be that friend."

"Are you going to tell Dad what I did?"

Eddie ran his hand through his mess of curls. "Nah. Not if this is the only time."

"Thanks." Douglas was pretty sure Eddie wouldn't tell on him, even if it did happen again. "Oh, you left a glass out, by the way. I poured it down the sink in case

Dad came down and saw it. Hope it wasn't the expensive stuff."

Eddie looked around the room to make sure ear shot was clear. "Never is. But thanks," he said. "It was a rough day."

Douglas barely mumbled a reply. He was trying to decide whether to ask the question that had been hiding behind the rest of his conversation with Eddie. He almost didn't, but Eddie turning to go seemed to trip something inside of him. "Hey . . . you didn't happen to come back last night after you left?"

Eddie's raised eyebrows almost hit his hairline. "Huh? Last night? No way. A midnight monster movie was on. Two buses full of cadavers couldn't have pulled me away from that. Spook yourself?"

"Yeah, I guess."

"That's not like you. But the morgue at midnight can do that to a person. That's why I suggest you never sneak down there so late again. Also, because your father will kill you, and even with my talents, I'm not so sure I could make you look pretty enough for your funeral after he's done with you."

Douglas lingered a few more moments over Marvin. He didn't really want to leave the coffin. It was almost as if as long as he could see the body—as long as it wasn't put into a hole with a piece of granite at its head—the murder wasn't complete. Marvin was still here.

The buzz of the attendees pulled Douglas back. He had hung out too long with the dead. He turned to assume his position at the door and almost ran right into a tall woman in glasses and a green dress with large flowers that seemed to want to be on a different dress or a different woman—the woman from Mr. Stauffer's funeral.

"What is your name?" The voice drifted above his head as the woman hovered over him like a guillotine. She had a weird little hat made of netting and black canvas pinned to the too-tight spirals of her brown hair.

"Douglas."

"Douglas what?"

"Douglas Mortimer."

"Mortimer as in Mortimer Family Funeral Home?"

"Yes, ma'am."

"You live here?"

"Yes, ma'am."

"That seems unwholesome for a boy your age."

"I don't know." The woman didn't seem ready to get out of his way. Suddenly he felt a tap on his shoulder.

"Hey, Doug, your dad wanted me to tell you he needs help with the refreshments."

"Thanks. Sorry, ma'am. Gotta go."

As soon as the two boys were far enough past the woman, Lowell snorted. "Coffee-drinker."

"Thanks for that. Hope she doesn't realize that there are no refreshments at this service."

"Eh, who cares. Who was she?"

"I don't know. She kept asking me questions. Said that living here was unwholesome for a boy my age. Not sure what she meant by that." Douglas squinted in thought.

"File it with the other 'who cares' topics." Lowell's hair looked like he had barely walked within fifteen feet of the nearest comb, and his shirt needed ironing. And replacing. Douglas couldn't blame him. After the night's scare, they'd both decided it was too risky for Lowell to head home right away, so he'd crashed on Douglas's floor for a few hours before sneaking out at first light when it felt safer . . . or at least more dangerous for his father to catch him than a killer.

"I checked online at school. Couldn't find any words that started with an *M* and *S*. Lowell punctuated the statement with a yawn large enough to crack his jawbone.

Douglas returned the reflex. He'd managed a relatively untroubled nap after school, but still felt the effects of last night's adventure.

"Maybe it's an abbreviation."

"Yeah, there are a bunch of those—Master of Science, Mississippi, multiple sclerosis. It's also a title somewhere between Miss and Mrs. Nothing that really makes sense to me, though. It could be from another language, too."

"Yeah. Well, here. Help me hand out programs."

Once the service was underway, Lowell found a seat and assumed a position that could hide his heavy eyelids. Perched on a folding chair at the back of the chapel, Douglas thought that maybe he had lost a battle with his own sleepiness and was dreaming the service. Everything seemed weird.

At the podium, Reverend Ahlgrim was eulogizing Marvin, but the O's in his speech seemed deflated. Douglas's parents, each standing in a back corner, seemed to be fidgeting beyond what they usually tolerated in the name of funeral decorum. Marvin's parents were in the front row, neither grieving audibly, each stuck in a wave of shock that wouldn't break for probably a few more days. Every once in a while, the woman in the flower print dress and tiny black hat turned around and looked at Douglas.

There was something unwholesome about this whole situation.

SEPTEMBER 24

SATURDAY

CHAPTER 10

Douglas leaned on the narrow sill of his bedroom window, immersing his head in the cool night. It was past midnight, just barely September 24, and just barely autumn. During the day, the season was announcing itself with the glorious colors of dying foliage. At night, it was proclaiming its presence through chill breezes, subdued owl hoots, and the quiet scraping of tree limbs.

Douglas nervously twisted an old-fashioned silver-handled cane in his hands. He was about to go out into that dark night. And he wasn't quite sure why.

Lowell had called him that morning. It had been three days since the funeral of Marvin, the murder victim.

"Let's sneak out to the cemetery tonight." Lowell was barely intelligible through bites of his breakfast cereal and blaring of a cartoon in the background.

"What?"

"The cemetery. Tonight. Sneak. Us."

"Why?"

"Well, I don't know if we ever need a reason to sneak out to the cemetery, but in this case, I've got something to tell you."

"Last time we did that, Cowlmouth got a murderer. I don't think I want any more news from you."

"Oh, but this is some news."

"Did your dad catch him?"

"Nope. But there's something new about the killer." Lowell clanged his spoon against his bowl in time to a commercial on the television. "Something nobody knows yet except the police and me. Something that's pretty important."

"What is it?" Douglas was still uncomfortable with how excited Lowell was over the murders.

"Tonight. At the cemetery."

"No way. Not with that creep still out there."

"We're perfectly safe tonight."

"How do you know?"

"You'll find out. Tonight. At the cemetery."

The conversation went on like that for another few minutes, until Douglas finally promised to meet Lowell.

As he peered out his bedroom window, Douglas was confident that Lowell wasn't lying about their safety. Douglas didn't think Lowell had ever lied to him, but that might mean that his friend was simply a great liar. Still, he'd stake his life on the fact that Lowell would never intentionally deceive him. *I guess I'm about to do that now,* Douglas thought. Of course, Lowell could've been plain wrong about his information.

That's why he was holding an old man's cane. The long shaft was made of dark oak, and was topped by a long flourish of silver cross-etched into a satisfying grip. Or a satisfying club-end, as that was how Douglas intended on using the cane tonight. Of all the midnight trips to the graveyard he'd taken in his life, this was the first time he felt he had to arm himself. The cane had belonged to a dead man. Probably still did. It was supposed to have been buried with one of the bodies at the funeral home a few years back, but at the last minute the widow of the deceased had decided she really wanted him to look like he was sleeping and asked them to change out his suit and favorite cane for a pair of pajamas. She even had them remove his glasses. She had never come back to claim his effects. The cane eventually ended up magpie-like in Douglas's room, where it leaned in a corner quietly predicting that Douglas would live to an age old enough to use it. The cane had become as much a comfort as a weapon.

Douglas was at his side window, the one that overlooked the parking lot. The one that was best for sneaking. With his head leaning slightly outside, as it was now, he could get a pretty good view of the front of the property, all the way to the dogwoods that lined both sides of the street and the large, old houses that hid behind them on the far side. Right now, though, he was gazing at the parking lot, which currently stabled the two vehicles that made up the Mortimer Family Funeral Home fleet along with Christopher's red jalopy. All three cars were in the appropriate spaces, each marked with a RESERVED sign. That meant everyone was home.

Douglas hoped there wouldn't be a removal call tonight. It was late, but people died at all hours, so there was always a chance that Christopher or his father would be up and preparing to pick up a body.

Lowell had been strangely specific about what time they were supposed to meet: 12:30 on the dot. It was just about that time now. Douglas spent a few more minutes summoning the courage to clamber down the outside of the house to the ground. His courage wasn't listening to him, though, remaining stubbornly hidden.

Normally, Lowell and Douglas met at the cemetery on their sneaks. Tonight, though, they'd agreed to meet outside Douglas's house and walk over together. Actually, *agreed* wasn't really accurate. Douglas had forced Lowell to meet him at his house as part of his terms. Regardless of Lowell's inside information, Douglas didn't want to walk to the cemetery by himself at night. These days, he seemed to see the shadow of the monster everywhere he looked: down alleyways; in closets; in empty classrooms . . .

Or right there.

A dark form was lurking across the street behind the dogwoods. Douglas thought for a second that it might be Lowell, but that wasn't the direction of his friend's house. And the figure was too tall. Douglas gripped the cane tighter.

"Doug." The single word made his heart squeeze down into a solid lump inside his rib cage.

Douglas didn't move until he heard his name repeated. He saw Lowell standing there with his hands cupped around his mouth. Douglas looked again at the line of trees across the street, but there was nothing there but the slender strips of trunk spaced evenly like bars on a zoo cage. He wasn't sure what he'd seen, but he sure didn't want Lowell to keep whisper-shouting his name.

Grabbing the rope ladder that his parents had nailed to his sill for fire emergencies, and carefully unrolling it down the side of the house, he shinnied down to meet Lowell, who was dressed in black sweatpants and a matching sweatshirt, with a black knitted cap covering the messy golden halo of his hair. It was perfect camouflage for the night . . . except that on his back was a bright green backpack with cartoon frogs all over it.

"It's my kid brother's. The strap on mine broke this afternoon."

"You going to use that Monday at school?"

"No way. Just tonight when I'll be with someone I can easily beat up if he makes fun of it."

Douglas laughed quietly and reached up for the knot in his tie, only to drop his hand when it came up against naked Adam's apple. Ties weren't sneaking attire. Like Lowell, he had on a dark sweatshirt, although he had settled on blue jeans and had a dark jacket to ward off the chill. He didn't need a cap. Douglas' dark head of hair melted into the night as if that's where it'd come from in the first place. The three strands of stiff hair angled across his forehead made it look like the darkness was running down his face.

His laughter stopped suddenly when he caught sight of the line of dogwood trees again; they seemed more ominous to him now that he was at ground level.

"Hey, do you see anything over there?" He nodded toward the trees.

"Trees, darkness, street lamp. Lots of stuff."

"Hmm."

"Anything wrong?"

"No, I guess not. Spooked myself while I was waiting for you."

"Man, I told you, we're safe tonight." Lowell eyed the cane in Douglas's hands, but said nothing. Douglas saw the taped hilt of a bat sticking through the top of Lowell's backpack. His friend had come similarly prepared. "Plus, you live in a funeral home. I thought that made you immune to being spooked. It's like your superpower, or something."

Douglas gave his friend a serious look while simultaneously trying to ignore Lowell's ridiculous backpack.

"Aren't you at all scared that there's a murderer running around town?" As soon as he said the M word, he regretted it. It wasn't the kind of word you said out loud in the dark.

"Sure . . . to a point. But Dad'll find him. Until then, it's kind of exciting. How often do people get an actual bad guy in life? Let's go."

The walk was nerve-wracking for Douglas, even after they got beyond the dogwoods, but it remained uneventful. Once they entered the towering gothic gates of Cowlmouth Cemetery, Douglas felt safe again. He always did. Nobody except for Moss and Feaster knew the cemetery better than he and Lowell did.

Cowlmouth Cemetery at night was a particularly special place. This late, he could believe all the stories of monsters that Moss and Feaster fed him as they buried the dead. Tombstones seemed to glow in the moonlight, as though they were having trouble holding back their ghosts. Mausoleum doors turned into gaping maws grown hungry since their last feeding. All the statues seemed to come alive: the grieving women, the saviors and angels, the animals.

Sometimes, the stories of monsters scared Douglas a little, not that he'd ever admitted that to anybody, and not so much that it ever stopped him from visiting the cemetery at night. Tonight, however, these monsters—the ones that populated his imagination—kept out that other monster—the one that was leaving mysterious marks in its victims.

Moss and Feaster had locked the front gates at dusk as usual, but the stone side walls were only about four feet tall, easy enough to climb over. As soon as they'd conquered one, both boys turned on their flashlights. Lowell led Douglas through the maze of funerary art deep into the cemetery to a large flat gravestone shaped like a tree stump. The name on it was R.T. Foard. It was one of at least six in the cemetery, all marking the graves of members of some sort of secret society: the Woodsmen, Douglas remembered somebody telling him once.

As they arrived at the strange grave marker, Lowell unslung the frog-covered backpack and set in on the top of the stump. As it hit the stone with a soft thump, green lights sewn into the backpack lit up and the whole thing erupted in a loud bull frog croak. Lowell cursed and started unzipping the pack.

Behind him, a twelve-foot-tall obelisk gave directions to the night sky, in case anybody needed them.

From this angle, the pillar seemed to be the center of the universe, the entire sky balancing on its point. It was dizzying.

Suddenly, Douglas felt all the bones in his skeleton freeze. Behind the obelisk, a shadow seemed to fidget furtively before slowly emerging. He tried to warn Lowell, but fear choked his throat.

The shadow came right for them.

CHAPTER 11

A person has quite a few options for reacting to an ominous shadow bearing down on him or her in a graveyard in the middle of the night. Douglas chose paralyzing terror and an awkwardly hefted cane. Lowell went with a friendly greeting.

"Hey, what's up?"

As he spoke, he pulled a small florescent lantern out of his little brother's backpack, hit the ON switch, and set it down on top of the stone tree stump. It flickered to life after a few seconds, lighting up a small area around the tombstone and making the rest of the cemetery even darker by contrast. As the shadow entered the luminous circle, it took the form of a girl.

She was casually holding a wicked-looking knife with a black blade and bright orange handle. She was about Douglas's height with straight black hair, an oversized dark brown jacket, and a purple ring that looked black in the soft lantern glow. Douglas decided to stick with paralyzing terror.

"Hey, Low," returned the girl, folding her knife with a snap and shoving it in her jacket. Douglas saw the blue asterisk of an emergency medical services insignia on its handle before it disappeared. "This Doug? Where's his tie?"

"Probably hanging neatly on a rack in his closet with about three dozen others." Lowell turned to Douglas. "Doug, this is Audrey Maudlin. She's in my class. I told you about her. Her dad's an ambulance driver, remember? Actually, I'm sure you do."

Douglas shot Lowell a look that roughly translated into an IOU for a punch in the neck.

Lowell ignored it and turned back to the new arrival. "You didn't bring a flashlight?"

Audrey retrieved a small orange one from a pocket in her jacket and held it up. "Turned it off when I got close. Wanted to make sure you guys weren't grave robbers or murderers or something."

"Yup," Lowell replied, "Just us guys. The grave robbers reserved a spot three rows over."

Audrey looked around at the few tombstones that the lantern illuminated and the pressing blackness of the cemetery beyond. "Do you guys do this often?"

"All the time," replied Lowell. "This is like our kingdom. Here, let me give you a quick tour." Lowell used his bat as a pointer. "The chapel is that way—it's got a great crypt beneath it. There's a covered bridge over there if you want to cross the stream without getting wet. And the only unlocked mausoleum in the entire place is over . . . there. The Grassley mausoleum. It's great for hiding, because nobody else in the entire town knows that it's unlocked, not even the cemetery caretakers." Lowell paused and aimed his bat at Audrey. "Please don't tell anybody about it."

Douglas spoke up. "What are you doing here?"

She shrugged. "Not sure, honestly. I guess I came here to find out why I came here." They both turned to Lowell.

"I think it's going to take all three of us to catch this serial killer."

"Serial killer?" Douglas asked.

"Yup. There've been two victims, and he's probably planned more. He's a serial killer."

"That's an ugly phrase. Remind me to congratulate him on his promotion, though," said Audrey. Douglas looked at her, and she dropped her eyes to the ground, embarrassed.

Suddenly, Douglas realized he'd asked the completely wrong question. "Wait, Lowell, you expect us to . . . catch . . . the murderer—serial killer?"

"Hot cider." Lowell reached into the backpack and pulled out a metal thermos and three plastic cups, ignoring both the croaking noise the movement triggered and the strange look from Audrey. "Autumn blood." He filled the cups and passed them around.

After taking a little too long and then waiting even longer while everybody had a sip, he finally said, "We won't catch him. But we can help."

"How?" asked Audrey.

"By keeping our eyes open during the day, sneaking out at night, and trying to figure out what's going on. By investigating."

"Why aren't we leaving this to your dad?" asked Douglas.

"We are, but we can't completely trust the coffee-drinkers. This guy's already killed two people on their watch. Who knows? Maybe the next victim will be one of our classmates. It's up to us."

"I can't see that there's very much we can do, other than get in trouble," said Audrey.

"And we certainly will do that, but there's other stuff besides trouble that we can get into. We have two things going for us. One, we're kids. We can be in places and find out things no adult can. Most coffee-drinkers don't even see us unless we break something or get in their way. The second element going for us is access to information. My dad's the police chief. Doug's is the mortician. You're the spawn of an ambulance driver, and that answers your question about why I invited you here tonight."

"Aren't we just a bunch of ghastlies," mumbled Douglas.

"We keep our eyes and ears open, and we sure as hockey sticks will learn something. For instance," Lowell took another sip of his cider and looked at each of them before continuing. "I know what the letters mean."

Douglas glanced quickly at Audrey. Lowell caught his look. "I told her about the letters already. Tell Doug what you told me."

"Just that I hope this guy isn't trying to put together the alphabet. That'd be a lot of dead people."

"She called him the Sesame Street Killer." Lowell laughed. "But the good news is, he's not," Lowell reached into the backpack again, gingerly this time to avoid setting off the electronic frog, and pulled out a small calendar, the type they give away free at local businesses. This one said "Mortimer Family Funeral Home, Est. 1809." Beneath the name and year was the slogan, "Rest for the Departed, Relief for the Bereaved." Lowell looked at Douglas. "Swiped it." He laid the calendar on the stump. "Check this out. Do you know when Mrs. Laurent was killed?"

Douglas looked at the calendar. "I'm not sure. I know her funeral service was on September 17."

"According to my father, she was killed five days before the funeral. That would be . . ." His index finger hovered above the open calendar until he found the appropriate white square. "A Monday. Marvin was killed on September 24. That's a Saturday. See what's happening?"

It was Audrey who got it first. "He's marking the days that he kills them on their faces."

"Exactly. M for Monday. S for Saturday. Which is why we're all perfectly safe being out here tonight, since, as of about an hour ago, it's officially Saturday."

"He already has this day of the week," added Douglas, who couldn't help but think, *It's still M for monster.* "Wait. How do they know?"

"Forensics, man. They know the exact hour of their death. And Mrs. Laurent and Marvin were both killed on the same day that they were found."

"Why would this guy do that?"

"Who knows? Why would he kill anybody in the first place? We're dealing with a psycho. A lot of *why's* don't have answers. But my dad says that killers often follow some kind of twisted logic, so it's worth thinking about. If we can figure out why he's matching up his kills with the days of the week, maybe that will help us figure out how to stop him. Or help the police stop him, at least."

That sounded like what Douglas's father had told him. Mr. Mortimer had said that the important thing was that the killer be punished, put somewhere that he won't be a danger to anybody. Douglas wondered if his father thought it so important that he'd be okay with having his twelve-year-old son running around at night with an old man's cane looking for the serial killer. Still, the monster needed to be stopped. Lowell had that part right.

"Are you sure he's not just marking the random days when he gets a victim? So he doesn't care if he gets two Mondays or three Thursdays or whatever?" asked Douglas, looking around and then trying to hide his nervousness. "Or maybe we're missing letters. I mean, victims. Either way, that would mean we're not safe tonight. Or any night."

"No to both. First, serial killers are collectors, not record keepers. Those marks are a message, and they're telling us that he's going to kill again, and when."

"Collect all seven," said Audrey.

"Right. And since the marks are messages, they're meant to be received. He makes sure his victims are found."

"And this is what your dad and the rest of the police think?"

"Yup. Got most of this straight from the vent itself. The vent is never wrong."

"I don't know. Sounds as if you plan to make us all *not* safe." Douglas didn't think that he, personally, was dealing very well with the idea of a killer. Everybody else seemed to be doing fine, though.

"No, we'll be okay. We'll have to be careful, but we'll be okay. Mostly, we'll come out on the nights that he's not dangerous."

"His days off?" asked Audrey.

"Right, his days off. Mondays and Saturdays . . . as of right now, anyway. He won't kill again on those days."

"Like hunting a vampire during the day," said Douglas dubiously.

"I guess that's a Moss-and-Feaster way of putting it. It sounds like a good idea, though, right?"

Audrey looked at him, half smiling, half shaking her head. "You mean it sounds like a fun idea. Two different things."

Douglas had always thought that one day something Lowell half-heard from his hallway vent was going to get them into real trouble.

Tonight looked like that night.

As Douglas watched Lowell disappear into the darkness, he saw a flash of green light and heard a quiet croak that was followed by another of Lowell's curses. Douglas flipped the cane upside down against his shoulder and turned to cross the street to his home and the soft bed that awaited him.

A serial killer, the wildest idea Lowell had ever come up with. Strangely, Douglas's mind alternated between murderers with calendar obsessions and Audrey. He wondered what kind of an impression he had made tonight. Brave? Whiny? He reached up to his neck and wished again he'd worn a tie, wished he'd called her by her name just once. He and Lowell had walked her to her house first before coming back here. It had been a good walk. Walking through the night, a friend on either side, danger on some far-off calendar square, it felt . . . like an adventure. Maybe's Lowell's crazy plan was worth going along with, for a little while at least. Despite the terrors of the night, both old and new, Douglas found himself comfortably lost in his own thoughts.

Until the dogwoods spoke to him.

Somewhere behind the ordered row of trunks, a short hiss of words seemed to connect the space behind him and them. They sounded hollow, inhuman, almost breaths.

He ran.

Ran like he'd never run in gym class, like no game of tag he'd ever played in the cemetery. Cold terror is the best fuel for the body.

Douglas didn't dare look back. Didn't even dare try to use the cane, which suddenly seemed silly in his hands. His breath came out ragged, and his feet slapped the ground even harder as he raced across the street to the front lawn of the funeral home. As he ran, he thought he could hear echoes of those sounds behind him. So close behind.

He ran even faster.

The night silhouette of the funeral home quickly loomed above him—a scary place for some, a safe harbor for him.

He dropped the heavy metal flashlight and the cane to the grass and grabbed onto the ladder dangling from his window. Loose rope tied around wooden rungs wasn't the best for speedy ascents, but Douglas took off up the ladder like a NASA launch, not worrying about the noise of the ladder slats hitting the siding of the house and hoping it woke everybody up—his family, Chris, every dead person in the morgue, the whole neighborhood, all of Cowlmouth itself. He hoisted himself through the open window, collapsing in terror.

His first thought as he hit the hardwood floor was *Pull the ladder up, idiot.*

With great effort, he reached out the window, and in the seconds that his head crossed the sill, saw below what looked like a black form. He squeezed his eyes shut, as though he were trying to get past the worst parts of a scary movie. He didn't want to see what was down there. What was looking up at him. What was climbing the ladder for him.

He yanked desperately at the ladder. It came up easily. No one was on it.

Douglas finally opened his eyes and looked down. All he saw on the ground below was the long metal tube of a darkened flashlight and the black stripe of cane laying across each other like crossbones in the grass.

CHAPTER 12

The blanket twisted into a serpentine shape, wrapping itself around Douglas's neck and chest and legs, trapping and constricting him in loops of anaconda cotton. His pillow, drenched in sweat, was a sucking, swallowing bog. His body wrestled with the horrible bedding throughout the night, while inside his skull, his mind wrestled with nightmares.

Images of a pale face wreathed in a dark aura looked up at him from below the window as he stared down in terror until he found himself slowly falling into it. Something metal and wicked glinted in one of the fiend's hands, and it traced letters of fire in the air. Then Douglas was racing futilely up the ladder, rungs breaking like chalk, the rope rails swaying crazily like the tails of living things, gravity pulling at him with mighty hands, every force in the universe bent on him not reaching the safety of his bedroom window. The monster's hand tugged his foot, and then Douglas dream-shifted into his bedroom. He felt a soft thump against his foot and, looking down, saw his own head looking up at him from the bedroom floorboards, seven letters scarring his cheeks and forehead.

All night, Douglas writhed in this fever of fear, and the next morning when his mother came to wake him, she needed no thermometer evidence to let him stay in bed.

During the day, the nightmares slowly dissipated, burned off by the rising sun, leaving him finally able to sleep.

He woke shortly before noon, leveraged himself out of the bed, threw on the same shirt and pants he'd worn the day before, and zombie-walked down the hallway to the kitchen, where he found his mother leaning against the counter with a cup of coffee in one hand and a phone in the other.

"Hello, Sweetie. How are you feeling?" she asked without looking up from the tiny screen.

"Horrible." Douglas dropped down into one of the hard, wooden chairs and laid his head on a place mat on the table that had an image of a bright red rooster. From Douglas's current vantage the image was distorted and dragon-like.

"How about some food?" she asked. "I picked up some fried chicken. Think you can handle that?"

"Yes." *Tell her.*

"You want it warmed-up or cold?"

"Cold, please." *Tell her.* "Where's Dad?"

"He's at the hospital taking care of some business." She slipped him a plate with two drumsticks and a large mound of mashed potatoes in the shape of the Styrofoam container that had held them and then poured him a soda, her bracelets clinking the entire time. She dropped a bendable straw into the drink. "You missed the Emmons funeral this morning."

Douglas was surprised to discover that he didn't care. He dug a hole in the smooth pile of mashed potatoes with a spoon.

"I saved you a program. It's up on your desk."

"Thank you." *Tell her.*

Suddenly, the phone in her hand buzzed hard enough that she almost dropped it into the grease-stained cardboard bucket that held the rest of the dismembered chicken. Douglas ignored the half of the conversation he could hear and stared at the pieces of chicken, picking at some of the crinkled skin half-heartedly. He should tell her. He wanted to tell her. *Mom, I think I was chased by a monster last night.*

"Okay. It'll take me a little bit of time." Mrs. Mortimer pushed a button on the phone, then turned to Douglas. "I've got to go do a removal in Singsburg. Will you be all right here by yourself for a little while?"

"Yes. I'll be fine." *I won't be fine.* "Where's Chris?"

"He's off tonight. Not sure where he is." She walked over and put a hand on her son's forehead. Douglas felt the metal of her rings pressing cold into the thin skin of his skull. "You don't feel hot. But maybe you should come with me."

"No. That's okay. Is Eddie downstairs?"

"I don't think so. I can call and ask him to come over. Or maybe Lowell."

"No, I'll watch some TV or something. I'll be fine." *The monster will come back to get me in this big, old, empty house.*

She tousled his hair and left to get ready. He automatically brushed it back into place, the three strands

138

assuming their usual positions like dutiful soldiers. He didn't know why he didn't tell her. In the kitchen, with a plateful of fried chicken, the rooster-dragon place mats, and the familiar jangle of his mother's jewelry, the events of last night didn't seem real. Maybe the whole thing had just been a nightmare. Maybe it all happened after he was safely in bed. He certainly had heard enough on that Woodsman's stump to inspire a few pillowcases full of nightmares.

No. Something had happened. He could walk up to his room, look out the window, and see a cane and a flashlight on the lawn like the used-up artifacts of some mysterious ceremony. He wanted it all to go away. The murderer, death, the coffins downstairs, the whole entire funeral business. He sighed and bit a mouthful of dead fowl. He'd feel better tomorrow. He would tell his mom then. And deal with everything else later.

Twenty minutes after his mother had left for the removal, Douglas was still in the kitchen with his cold chicken and colder thoughts. He'd just decided to shine the comforting light of a television screen into the darker corners of his brain when the back door's bell rang. It was a harsh buzz, distinct from the comforting chimes of the funeral home's downstairs.

A sickeningly familiar feeling bloomed in the pit of his stomach. It was a sharp reminder of how not-dream last night was. The doorbell rang again. *Wait. Do murderers ring doorbells?* That didn't seem right. The doorbell rang again. And again. Then it starting buzzing in a weird, random pattern. If there was a most annoying way to ring a doorbell, this was it. And that thought is what finally made him realize who was at the back door. It wasn't the monster.

"Hi, Low."

"Whoa, Doug. It looks like you left most of yourself in bed," Lowell said as he breezed into the house, followed closely by Audrey.

Douglas immediately wished that he'd put on fresh clothes and cleaned up so that he didn't look like a pre-Eddie corpse. "What are you guys doing here?"

"Your mom called and asked me to come over. Figured I'd get the Ghastlies together while I'm at it. Is that fried chicken?" Lowell liberated a thigh and a leg from the waxed cardboard bucket, keeping the thigh for himself and throwing the leg at Audrey's head. She caught it with one hand and took a massive bite out of the meat. Lowell leaned against the counter, gnawing on the thigh like he'd grown up during a famine.

"Is it okay that we came? I mean, if you're sick . . ." Audrey spoke between mouthfuls of chicken.

"No, it's fine. I'm glad you came." Douglas looked around quickly. "I'm glad you guys are here. I need to tell you something."

"Is that where the funeral home part is? Right under us? Can we go down and see it?" Audrey was standing at the top of the stairs that led down to the family business.

"Uh . . . " started Douglas before Lowell quickly cut in.

"Definitely. It's awesome down there. You should see the coffin room."

"Coffin room? Let's go."

Lowell and Audrey threw their chicken bones onto a rooster place mat and took off pounding down the stairs. It took a few more beats for Douglas to follow.

As he hit the bottom, he heard Audrey blurt out, "That is a lot of coffins. Crazy. And he sleeps upstairs?"

Audrey and Lowell were chest-deep in floating coffins, smudging brass and wood with fingers greased from chicken, peering into the depths of the boxes like they were looking for future occupants.

Audrey saw Douglas come around the corner. "Hey,

Doug, what's the difference between a coffin and a casket anyway?"

"Coffins are thinner at the feet than at the shoulders and caskets are more rectangular. We use the words the same way here, because we mostly sell caskets, but don't want to confuse the bereaved."

"Coffin is a much cooler word," said Lowell.

"Look at this one," Audrey continued as if she hadn't even heard his answer. She was placing both her hands on a massive coffin that seemed big enough to fit two people. The dark exotic wood glowed with gold dust and was ornamented by a luxurious array of gold fittings and ivory inlays in the shapes of birds and sunbursts.

"That's the Splendor 4000. It's pretty expensive. I don't think anybody's ever bought one before."

Lowell piped up. "I've always told Doug that he should convince his dad to stick some wheels on it and let Doug drive it around."

"I suppose if you have to go, you might as well go out like this," she said, running her fingers along an ivory flock of birds.

"Ha. No way. Not for me," Lowell said. "See those pretty vases on the wall? That's how I want to go. Burn me to ashes. Shove me in a vase. Stick flowers in me.

Set me in the middle of the dining room table every Thanksgiving and Christmas."

Audrey moved to a cherry wood coffin and pressed the silk lining with the flat of her hand like she was feeling for a pea. "These are all pretty cool, even the plain ones. It's a shame they get buried." She paused. "Can I get in one?"

"No way," answered Lowell. "Me and Doug tried that once when we were kids. Knocked it onto the floor. Smashed one of its corners. We got in so much trouble." He paused. "Then again, there's three of us now, and we're much older. We could totally . . ."

"I think the murderer almost got me last night."

The room full of empty coffins suddenly seemed a lot more dead.

Lowell turned slowly toward him. "What?"

"The monster. The serial killer. After we split up, I think he chased me."

There was another long pause as Lowell and Audrey seemed to be adjusting their realities to fit this horrifying, overwhelming new piece of information. Lowell finally broke the silence.

"You think?"

"Yeah. I mean, I heard something, so I ran and I

think I was chased. I got into my room and then peeked out and thought I saw somebody, but I'm not sure. It was really dark." Douglas cringed as he realized how uncertain it all sounded out loud.

"That's all pretty vague," replied Lowell. "Besides, that's impossible. It's Saturday."

"Maybe you're wrong about the whole days of the week thing."

"I heard my father . . ."

"Maybe *he's* wrong."

"Maybe we have our *S* days confused," offered Audrey. "Maybe the second victim was a Sunday and he needed his Saturday."

Douglas looked at Lowell. Lowell slowly responded. "No. No. That Marvin guy was killed on a Saturday, and we didn't leave Doug's house until after midnight on Saturday morning. I made sure of that."

"Doug, have you told anybody?" asked Audrey.

"Not yet. I had a rough night and slept all morning. Plus . . ."

"Plus, he's not sure it happened," finished Lowell.

"Still, he should at least tell his parents."

Suddenly, a coffin door slammed shut. It was a startling sound to Douglas. Coffin lids were always gently lowered. But Lowell had done just that. He stood there beside the closed coffin, his eyes set in a hard stare. "Doug, did you see his face?"

"No."

"Is there anything you can tell the police? What was he wearing? Was he carrying anything? Did he say something?"

"I don't know." Douglas paused as if having a rapid conversation with himself before continuing, "I might have heard him say something, though."

"What?" asked Lowell.

"Maybe it was nothing."

Lowell grunted, then tried again. "Well, what do you think you heard?"

"Something about the sun, I think. Maybe 'sick of sun'? I'm really not sure."

"Sick of sun," repeated Lowell, looking around the coffin room as if he could find some kind of context for the phrase within all that merchandise of death.

"It could still be a calendar thing," said Audrey.

"What do you mean?" asked Douglas.

"Well, if he really is killing according to the days of the week, the sun could be some kind of reference to daytime. He might even have been saying, *Sunday*."

"All right," said Lowell, "Let's keep thinking about that. But, most important, we have no evidence we can take to your parents or my dad, right?"

"No . . . no." Douglas could barely contain a shiver at the memory of what little he could remember.

Lowell nodded. "In that case, we can't tell anybody. Not parents. Not police. We have to keep this to ourselves."

"What? Low, that's ridiculous," said Audrey, crossing her arms tightly in front of her, her ring catching light and flickering like purple fire. "We have to tell someone. To protect Doug and to let the police know that they might be wrong about this whole day of the week idea. They have to know."

"Listen," Lowell said. "We don't even know if he saw anything. Sorry, Doug, we just don't. It was a spooky night. We all get the creeps. Remember that night in the cemetery I saw a UFO?"

"Thought you saw a UFO," said Douglas.

"Exactly. And if you tell a coffee-drinker, the police will be no closer to finding this monster than they are if you don't tell them. We don't have anything new. Not a description of his face, nothing about his clothes, not a single piece of evidence that will help the investigation. And this day of the week thing . . ." Lowell stopped and looked down at the carpet. "I think maybe we timed it too tight. Or I did, anyway. It was only an hour from Friday. Maybe the killer doesn't care about being exact." He turned back to Douglas. "That was completely my fault. I didn't think about that. I'm sorry, man."

Douglas barely made eye contact with him—with either Ghastly, in fact. The whole conversation was making him uncomfortable.

"What about the 'sick of sun' clue?" interjected Audrey. "That's got to be worth something to the police."

Lowell shook his head. "I doubt it. If it *is* a day of the week reference, it's nothing we don't already know. It's not enough. Not enough to risk the consequences."

"Consequences?" asked Audrey.

"Thanks to this monster on the loose, all the coffee-drinkers are already overprotective of us. I mean, for goodness sake, my dad is working the night shift tonight, and he hired a babysitter to stay with me and my brother. He's never done that. I'm almost fourteen! It made it really hard to sneak out last night. If the coffee-drinkers hear about us poking around in this, it'll be worse than an entire summer of grounding.

"More important, we won't be able to help catch the monster. He might get away. Kill even more people. There are five more days in this killer's week. Five more people who could die. We can't let that happen. So we mistimed last night. It's not a mistake we'll make again." He turned to Douglas. "I mean it, Doug. Nothing good will come of telling the coffee-drinkers. I mean, wish I would have stayed with you last night until you got inside, but from now on, we'll be a whole lot more careful. Never leave each other alone. And we can always tell my dad later if we have to. But for now, we can't . . . tell . . . anybody."

The three friends looked at one another in silence, surrounded by coffins in a town tainted by murder. Douglas looked up at the urns and imagined his grandmother's photo glaring down in disapproval.

The sudden sound of a door slamming and keys landing loudly on a countertop told them one of Douglas's parents had returned.

OCTOBER 1

SATURDAY

CHAPTER 13

"The killer is definitely here." Lowell shaded his eyes with his hand in the late morning sunlight as he surveyed the tableau in front of him. Behind him, the large jaws of a monster threatened to devour him in a single bite.

"Yeah, everybody's here," said Douglas.

The Ghastlies stood on a rise at one end of the fairgrounds. As far as they could see, the world was covered in golden tents that looked as if they had sprung up wherever a falling leaf had hit the ground. Where there wasn't a tent, there were massive machines spinning and shaking, moving up and down, swinging back and forth. The rides looked as if they had been put together yesterday, but also like they had been standing there making those same movements for eons. People filled the spaces in between like they were the first modern humans allowed to visit a newly discovered jungle city or some ancient metropolis dug out from millennia of dry lava or pulled fresh from the ocean where it had sunk.

The sounds that gave the new and ancient tent city life were terrible: barn animal brays and snorts and bleats; clangs and clatters and bells and screams and yells from rides and games; tinny, repetitive music forced out of beat-up speakers. Horrible noises, one and all, that together swelled into mysterious harmonies so invigorating that nature and town both shut up and deferred to it.

As giddy as the sights and sounds were, it was the smells that really defined the carnival. Had the mythical sirens been bakers instead of singers, this is the aroma that would have driven sailors mad: fresh, sugared dough and cotton candy so thick and sweet it confused the bees into trying to help pollinate the fluffy pink flowers on their white stems. Sausages so savory and greasy they needed no mustard, no bun, just a coat of aluminum foil to keep them warm and keep fingers clean. Heaping lobster rolls so buttery, bright, and delicious that it was inconceivable that they came from some mere bottom-feeder out of the dark ocean. Spiced apple cider and pumpkin pies and onion rings like Saturn's own, and turkey legs the size of dinosaur bones. It was all enough to pull a grown man nose-first through the air like a cartoon character.

The Cowlmouth Fall Carnival was like an aligning of the planets. Everything was right about it.

Except for the murderer that some unsuspecting ticket taker had allowed onto the grounds.

Douglas, Lowell, and Audrey had met about half an hour earlier, at the monster with the wide-open maw. Its face was black, with spiral eyes, long red horns that almost touched at the top, and a red and pointy nose. Its mouth was large enough to swallow all three Ghastlies without having to wash them down. Tattooed on the tractor trailer body of the monster was a chaos of evil creatures in faded comic book colors that would have tested the bounds of the collected knowledge of Moss and Feaster. Pale letters like ghosts drifted through the fangs and claws and scales and scowls, dubbing the dark ride THE SOUL TAKER.

The three friends had to squeeze into a tiny metal car that *clack-clack*ed them along a track, past the teeth of the demon, and into the total darkness of its gullet. First came the sounds: the driving music, the screams of victims and howls of their victimizers. The rain and thunder. The random bits of dialogue and maniacal laughter of long-dead black-and-white horror movie actors. Every jerky turn meant a sore neck and the revelation of some dimly lit piece of papier-mâché or cardboard monster that jumped out with a pneumatic hiss and a caterwaul. Every once in a while, fake lightning flashes revealed more intricate scenes, like plastic skeletons manacled to the wall or a decapitated mannequin in a cape pulling his own head from a magician's hat or a cannibal feast of rubber body parts. It took two minutes to get through the whole thing, and it was incredibly cheesy. They'd ridden it three times so far.

"What does a killer look like in the daylight?" asked Douglas.

"He probably has a mustache. Black and waxy and curled at the tips. He'll be twirling it," said Audrey.

"We're looking for somebody who's really scrutinizing the crowds, sizing everybody up," Lowell replied.

"Like we're doing," said Douglas.

"On the other hand, the killer could be in Dr. Jekyll mode. He could be somebody we're all familiar with, someone friendly, chatting everybody up and having a good time."

"Like we should be doing," said Douglas.

"Whoever he is," said Lowell, "There's a lot of carnival down there. We better get searching."

"I'll keep my eyes open, but I'm going to have to catch up with you guys later," said Audrey. "I have to meet my folks for pictures."

"Pictures?"

"Yeah, some booth is doing weird family photos or something. You know, everybody in cowboy hats or hula skirts in front of a green screen. Real dumb, so of course Dad and Mom want to do it."

"Well, that's a picture you should hope never gets around school, so don't let me get my hands on it. You want to meet up in, say, two hours over by the Ferris wheel?" asked Lowell.

As Audrey disappeared into the crowd, Douglas turned to Lowell. "Where should we start?"

"First things first." Lowell marched down the hill and into a corridor of food stands. Lining both sides of the wide, hard-packed dirt path were endless rows of vendors selling everything a person needed to both love and hate life. Lowell seemed to show little interest in the offerings as he strutted determinedly down the center of the path. Neither the soft pretzel seller nor the funnel cake vendor nor the popcorn stand snagged so much as a sniff from the lanky boy. At one point, they passed a small plywood booth advertising hot dogs. It was manned by a human-sized cardboard cutout of a familiar hot dog with arms, legs, and a creepy-happy face. A sign on the booth read, In Memory of Irwin Stauffer. This was the first Cowlmouth Fall Carnival that the hot dog vendor had missed in more than half a century.

Finally, Lowell veered from his course, heading for a simple-looking white food truck decorated with bright illustrations of apples on sticks. Embedded inside, as firm as a hermit crab in its shell, was a giant woman in a white apron. She had an anvil tattooed on one swollen forearm, like Popeye.

"What do you want?"

Lowell dropped some money on the counter and threw a fastball question over his shoulder. "Candy or caramel?"

"Caramel," said Douglas.

"Candy for me," Lowell said to Ms. Popeye. She handed the treats to Lowell, who grabbed them by their sticks. Douglas took his, a beautiful, smooth brown sphere, except at the bottom of the apple, where the excess caramel had run down its sides and congealed into a thick disc of sweet, enamel-ripping tar. Lowell's was bright red and had a face painted on it with icing and cookie bits, like a shrunken head right off the necklace of some Candy Land headhunter. He tore half the face off with one bite, a double crunch of candy coating and apple guts.

"So, what do you think?" With the apple chunks glued to the roof of his mouth by red cement, Lowell's voice sounded lower and his vowels came out funny. "Giant pumpkin tent or alpaca barn?" He suddenly froze, his eyes lifted as if they'd been tugged by a string. "Wait a minute . . . we're going there."

He used his half-eaten candy apple to point to a canvas sign strung across the roof of a tent: ODDITORIUM.

Once the boys got closer to the tent, they could see it was covered in illustrations of people . . . strange people: a man so skinny you could make out every bone in his skeleton; a little girl in a long-sleeved plaid dress and knee-high socks, her face covered in werewolf fuzz; a man whose torso was poked full of holes; a woman whose skin looked like tree bark.

At the entrance to the tent was a podium where a young man with long, greasy hair, wearing a T-shirt with a character from a thirty-year-old video game, stared down at the screen of a tablet computer. Lowell pulled out a snake of red tickets from his pocket and handed it to the man who took them without counting. Douglas did the same, but this time the man's eyes lifted from the screen. A smile stretched the ratty hair around his mouth, "Welcome to the freak show. No refunds."

As they passed through the half-open flap, it took a few moments for Douglas's eyes to adjust to the dim interior. His nose started collecting clues first. Formaldehyde. Alcohol. Old death. Rot. Familiar smells for Douglas. Nostalgic smells.

"Stinks bad in here," said Lowell, eyeing what remained of his candy apple dubiously.

Then they saw the jars.

Directly in front of them was an eight-foot high wall of shelves packed with glass jars of varying shapes. Each was filled with liquids—orange liquid, yellow liquid, brown liquid, clear liquid. Each glass container preserved a dead animal—a deformed dead animal. A piglet with two heads, a kitten with five legs, two ducklings joined at the breast, a bald mouse covered in small round nodules, a puppy with tusks jutting out of its muzzle. Not everything sunk within the jars was recognizable.

The preserved animal freaks continued down a maze of hallways like a house of mirrors, although instead of Douglas and Lowell seeing themselves in the glass, they saw a tortoise missing its top shell and a fish with an extra mouth halfway down its body and a gecko with three tails.

There were strange creatures outside of the jars, too—taxidermied specimens evolution had ruled out millennia ago: a pony sprouting a narwhal horn from its forehead; a bat with frog legs instead of wings; a ferret with a rattlesnake tail. Sometimes, the animals were immortalized in fanciful poses, like two bullfrogs dueling with tiny sabers or a guinea pig in a bonnet and glasses sitting in a guinea pig-sized rocking chair reading a guinea pig-sized book.

"Man, ain't no people in here. Just animals. Sort of," said Lowell.

Just death, thought Douglas, taking a bite out of his caramel apple. *Death on display.*

As they wandered the labyrinth of jars and sawdust-stuffed corpses, their disappointment at the false advertisement quickly evaporated.

"A squirrel with one eye!"

"There's a face on the back of that stingray!"

"No way that's a real worm. Look how long it is!"

And then a quiet question stranger than any of those exclamations.

"How are you feeling?"

Douglas turned to face Lowell, who had asked the question around the bare candy apple stick still in his mouth, while he bent down to examine a creature that looked like a shaved monkey torso sewn to a fish's tail. A paper placard labeled it a Feejee Mermaid. "I don't know. It's kind of cool. Kind of nauseating, too."

"I mean about last week. After the cemetery."

"Oh, that. I'm okay." Each day since their cemetery visit seemed to push the nightmares father away. Now they were merely the monster-stalking-town sort of nightmares instead of the monster-personally-had-it-out-for-him sort. Douglas was becoming a nightmare connoisseur.

The few intervening days had done little to resolve the argument in the showroom, though. The trio had since occupied themselves with what Lowell loved to call "patrolling" and "investigating," but what was, in reality, much closer to wandering and hanging out downtown at the shops or the movie theater, before they invariably found themselves back at the graveyard. Still, the quandary of whether to tell their parents was always present.

"Think we're doing the right thing?" Lowell leaned in closer to the mermaid as if he were trying to see the stitching in the dimness. The stick in his mouth quivered inches from the mermaid's features, which seemed to be peeled back in permanent horror.

"I don't know. We're definitely doing the scary thing." Douglas peered into one of the jars and saw a furry spider the size of a bowling ball floating inside.

"Well, the more I think about it, the more I think it's the right thing. Mostly because of you. If you are right about what happened that night, you might be the most important person in Cowlmouth right now."

"Why?"

"You're the only one to have gotten near the monster and lived. Sure, you don't remember anything useful about him, but who knows what might come to you under the right circumstances. Maybe you'll spot somebody in the crowd outside, and you'll recognize their vibe. Or you'll overhear somebody talking, and it'll sound like the voice you heard. Or you'll bump into the killer around the corner and he'll stare at you like you're a baby shark with feathers or something, and you'll suddenly know it's him. It's one of the reasons you need to be out in the open and not holed up in your house." Lowell was facing Douglas, his head framed by a large jar with something horned suspended inside. Douglas looked at his best friend like he was the weirdest thing in the entire tent. It took him a long time to respond.

"I never thought about that. I wish you hadn't made me think about that now."

"What do you mean?"

"If there's a small chance I might be able to recognize the monster here, there's a pretty large one that he'll recognize me. He's probably already seen me. He might even have followed us in here." Douglas was surprised at how matter-of-fact his voice sounded. His nightmares were apparently exhausting his ability to be terrified.

Lowell didn't have a response. The two boys stood there, surrounded by animal oddities, as cold inside as the things submerged in the jars.

"Maybe we should go somewhere less eerie," Lowell finally suggested.

"Maybe."

But Douglas's worry wasn't left behind with the beakless raven and the fox with the hawk wings. It followed him to the alpaca barn, where they watched a man shear one of the strange beasts of its wool coat in less than a minute. It followed him as they sat in the classic car lot, trying out horns and steering wheels. It followed him as they perched on the fence and watched the scarecrow-stuffing competition. It followed him as they passed the photo booth Audrey had mentioned, where a balding man with a mustache and glasses tried frantically to pose a family of seven in matching vampire capes and fangs so he could take their picture. It looked like a stressful job.

Everybody at the carnival seemed to be a fun house mirror reflection to Douglas—distorted versions of those whom he usually saw. Either they were killers or they were victims. Douglas wasn't sure which was worse.

"I wonder if any records were broken this year." The two friends were in line to see the bloated orange wonders of the season, the giant pumpkins. Lowell had a cinnamon-sprinkled sugar cookie the size of a hubcap in his hand. Douglas was dissolving a wasp nest of maple cotton candy in his mouth.

Douglas shrugged. "Last year, they had one that was almost three thousand pounds. That's like a ton and a half of pumpkin. That's going to be hard to beat." The giant pumpkins were Douglas's favorite part of the carnival. He loved those massive, misshapen fruits. Regular pumpkins were great. They were the defining feature of fall, spooky and comforting and delicious and disgusting. He couldn't imagine if the seasons had been different and the official fruit had ended up being a strawberry or a grapefruit or worst of all, a banana. But pumpkins—you could turn those bright orange globes into goblins with a few slices of a kitchen knife . . . and a few more is all it took to turn them into pies, to roast their seeds into crunchy, savory tooth-crackers. They were perfect.

Especially because you could grow them into giants.

About three-quarters of the way through the cookie and all the way through the cotton candy, the boys made it inside the large tent. The space was so full of giant pumpkins that it almost seemed as if the inside of the tent glowed orange. They wandered among the squash in awe, the way people walk through redwood forests or beneath the shadows of mountains. There were fat, wide pumpkins that you could sit on like hard chairs; tall, slumped ones that looked as if they had been frozen mid-melt; surreally-shaped ones that looked as though they'd erupted from the ground with a loud *bloop* instead of blossoming slowly at the end of vines. They had names like Cinderella's Coach and Peter Peter's Wife and Linus's Nightmare. Every single one was a glorious, swollen, ugly, beautiful, bloated dream-creature that could only live in the twilight season of fall.

The pumpkins were so massive, they had to be set on wooden pallets so that forklifts could pick them up to move them. Every once in a while, the boys would see a pumpkin farmer rubbing oil on the taut skin of one of the mini-planets, trying to avoid the cracks that would disqualify it from the competition.

Later, the winner would have the honor of carving his giant pumpkin into a monstrous jack-o'-lantern and setting it in the middle of downtown for Halloween night. The three runners-up would be taken to a field on the fairgrounds, hoisted up by a crane and dropped with an enormous explosion of pumpkin flesh. A few others would be carved into boats and paddled around the river.

Giant pumpkins were absolutely awesome.

Of course, this year, the thing that Douglas noticed most about them was how easily they could conceal somebody behind them. The rows of giant pumpkins were almost more eerie than the dim maze of jarred dead things in the Odditorium tent.

Suddenly, a terrible yell, almost a scream, ripped through the crowd.

"Somebody cut Jill! Somebody *cut* Jill!"

The crowd started surging toward and swirling around a single point in the tent like somebody had pulled a drain plug from its hole. Douglas and Lowell were borne along, but were able to take advantage of their smaller size to wriggle their way to the front.

A gray, grizzled man in a tractor cap and faded red sweatshirt was kneeling in front of the victim, weeping.

"Jill, Jill," the man kept repeating. He looked around at the gathering crowd "Who did this?"

In front of the man, the orange behemoth—JILL THE GIANT, according to a homemade poster decorated in orange and green marker—seemed unperturbed by his outpouring of sorrow and anger. Right in the middle of the pumpkin, a jagged *S* gaped in the orange flesh.

Aside from the pumpkin farmer, the individuals who seemed most unsettled by the act of vegetable vandalism were the two boys standing frozen behind him. They stood there while the rest of the crowd stared and whispered, and while most of the onlookers dispersed, and while the grieving pumpkin farmer stormed off to find a way to avenge Jill.

Finally, when the crowd had thinned, the boys were able to get closer to examine the latest victim.

"It looks like Martin's *S*," said Douglas in a low whisper.

"Yeah, just bigger. Same knife-writing for sure."

"Why would the killer slash a pumpkin?"

"There should be police tape around this thing."

Douglas reached out and traced the long angular letter. "I think this is a warning."

"A warning."

"Martin's *S* was for Saturday, this one must be for Sunday."

"Tomorrow."

"Exactly."

Lowell started pulling at the cuffs on his shirt. "It's kind of a strange warning. Most of Cowlmouth doesn't even know there's a letter-obsessed killer out there. You heard the crowd. They think kids did this."

"You said it yourself in the graveyard the other night. The killer wants his marks seen. That's why he's making them. So far, thanks to the police, nobody knows about them."

"So this is him . . ."

"Warning everybody holding onto the secret when the next murder will happen: Sunday. Tomorrow. Now the police have to let people know to protect them."

"Maybe. If the police even get this message."

Douglas nodded slowly. "You're right. I think it's up to us. We need to tell the police about this."

"Yeah, I guess we do. My dad's going to ground me until college."

Douglas plucked at the strands of hair streaking across his forehead like they were harp strings. "I think there might be another way. Come on."

He led Lowell through the bulbous orange rows and back out into daylight. "Look around. Do you see anybody that works for your dad nearby? Somebody that looks like they're not on duty?"

"This is a big carnival. Most of the force is here. Wait, there's PH." Lowell pointed at a solitary man hanging out near the backside of a tent. The man wore jeans, white sneakers, a thick hoodie adorned with a large football, and a ball cap with a baseball on it. "His name's Philip Hubbell, but he always makes me call him PH.

Why does it matter that he's not on duty? *Oooooooooh*."
Lowell smacked his forehead with the palms of his
hands. "I get where you're going with this. We just need
to casually place the information, all innocent-like. Let
me take us the rest of the way."

Lowell and Douglas approached the officer at an
angle that made it look like they were just happening to
pass by the man. "Hey, PH," said Lowell as they got close.

"Mr. Lowell Pumphrey. Enjoying the fair?" In one
hand, the officer held a paper cup with something steaming in it and a large cinnamon pretzel in the other.

"It's great." Lowell's voice suddenly sounded different to Douglas, like he was three years younger. "This is
my friend, Doug."

"Hello, Doug."

"Is your family here?" asked Lowell.

"They're here . . . somewhere. I think at the tractor
museum. I wanted to get a pretzel and a cider." He held
them up like they were evidence.

"I'll make sure I say hi if I see them. We just came
from the pumpkin tent across the way. Some big ones
over there."

"I'll bet. Did they announce the winner? I've got
twenty bucks on Pumpkinhead."

"No, not yet. But there was a big commotion in there. Apparently, somebody vandalized a pumpkin."

"I hope it wasn't Pumpkinhead."

"No, Jill the Giant. So is that like a crime? Just curious. Do you have to investigate it and treat it like a crime scene?"

"I'm off duty, kid. Just enjoying the fair. Tell you what, though. I'll make sure the Pumpkin Crimes Division handles it."

"Ha, Pumpkin Crimes Division. Anyway, whoever did it really messed the pumpkin up. The farmer was devastated. All because somebody carved their initial into its face."

Hubbell's own face suddenly went stony. "Yeah, that's too bad for the farmer." He knocked up the bridge of his cap with the rim of his cup. "Um, so what letter was the initial?"

"I think it was an *S*. Anyway, we're headed to the Ferris wheel, so I guess we'll see you around. Hope your pumpkin wins."

"Yeah, thanks. I'll talk to you later, Lowell."

Lowell and Douglas waited until they rounded the corner of a tent before they peeked back the way they'd come. Hubbell was halfway to the pumpkins, tossing his full cup of cider and barely nibbled pretzel into a trash can as he went.

"Let's go find Audrey," said Douglas.

The two boys took off through the carnival crowds. They ignored the insults of the carnies at their game booths as they passed through the midway. They didn't look twice at the sign announcing the world's largest horse and were oblivious to the loudspeaker proclaiming the world's smallest woman, "She's only twenty-nine inches tall! Her shoe size is a two! And her four sons are each over six feet tall!"

Audrey was waiting for them at the Ferris wheel when they got there.

"You two look like you have something to tell me."

"Man, do we," said Douglas. He began to explain, when he was interrupted by a couple of teenage girls behind them.

"Are you guys in line?"

"No," said Lowell.

"Yes," said Audrey, and then to Lowell and Douglas, "Let's go on the Ferris wheel." A few strange, silent seconds went by. Finally, she asked, "What?"

Douglas laughed. "Lowell's not a big fan of Ferris wheels."

"Are you scared of rides?"

"I'm not scared of rides," explained Lowell through clenched teeth. "I'll go shoulder-to-shoulder with you on any roller coaster. But I don't trust Ferris wheels. They creak and jerk and sway and go so slow they feel like they're breaking down every second. They're dumb."

"You sound scared. There's a carousel over there we can jump on. You can have first pick of the horsies."

"Are you guys getting on or what?" one of the teen girls asked impatiently. The Ghastlies found themselves at the front of the line. The Ferris wheel attendant had the gate open, but apparently didn't care whether anybody went through or not.

"Yes, in fact, we are," said Audrey as she strolled through the gate. Douglas followed, and Lowell reluctantly brought up the rear.

Douglas found himself in the middle of the car as the attendant fastened the metal safety bar across them with an awful creak. He looked at Lowell as the wheel jerked to life. He was holding onto the bar tight enough that it looked like he was trying to snap it in two.

"So what's going on?" asked Audrey.

"By tomorrow, the entire town will know about the serial killer," said Douglas.

"What?"

Douglas relayed the whole story of Jill the pumpkin and PH the policeman. By the time he'd finished, the three friends were swaying at the top of the Ferris wheel. Lowell hadn't said a word the entire time. The slight green tinge of his face clashed with the bright yellow of his hair. Below them, the entirety of the Cowlmouth Fall Carnival stretched like an autumn-colored utopia.

"So you think that the police will draw the same conclusion you are. And will have to tell everyone that there's a serial killer hunting on the streets of Cowlmouth."

"Right," said Lowell, jumping a bit as the car rocked gently in a breeze.

"If they sit on this warning and somebody dies tomorrow, well, that's bad," said Douglas.

"I wonder what that'll be like," said Audrey. "The entire town knowing what we've known for weeks."

"It's going to be weird," agreed Douglas, "But I think I'm going to like it."

"What do you mean?"

"I'll feel safer once everybody knows the danger. We won't be alone in this." He paused for a few seconds, thinking. "Although, it's funny. That'll be the opposite reaction of everybody else. They'll all be freaking out."

"The good news is it won't change things too much for us, since our parents already know about it," said Lowell, finishing the observation with a series of muttered curses as the car dipped down to the bottom and then kept going.

"I think there might be bad news in this, though," said Audrey. "Obviously, the pumpkin was mutilated very close to when you arrived at the tent. It means you were near enough to the psycho. That's concerning for you, Doug, because that's twice now. Seems a strange coincidence."

Douglas looked out over the carnival like all the answers could be found among the tents, the rides, and the games if he could just stay up in the air long enough to see them. "Yeah. There is that."

The Ferris wheel continued its revolutions.

OCTOBER 3

MONDAY

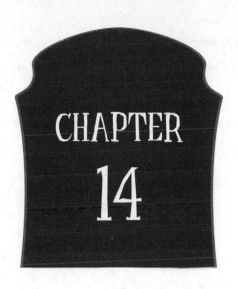

CHAPTER 14

Cowlmouth Library was erected to save the souls of men. Now it shaded their thoughts. The three hundred-year-old building had started its life as a church and was currently an official historical landmark. However, it needed some other purpose beyond being a field trip stop, so the town stuffed it to the holy rafters with books.

Nevertheless, it retained its imposing ecclesiastical qualities. It was incredibly tall at its tallest point, squat at its squattest, and wide at its widest. It was made of thick slabs of rough-hewn rain-gray granite the size of small cars and sported a white steeple that stretched into the sky above like it was being pulled thin by unseen fingers. It even had gargoyles. According to Moss and Feaster, these ugly, bat-winged hunks of masonry regularly turned to flesh and flew around the night skies of Cowlmouth, picking off stragglers caught out too late at night. Only a book in one's hand could ward off the flinty fiends.

"This feels weird." Lowell looked up at the stone monsters glaring down from their niches. "Like we're going back to school after just leaving it. Can't we ask your mom to drop us off at the movies instead?"

"We need to be here. Well, I need to be here. You can go to the movies, I guess."

"Shut up, man."

The two walked toward the front door of the library. It was large and red with black three-pronged hinges that looked like pitchforks. It had never been open since Douglas could remember. Beside the massive portal was a smaller modern glass entrance that automatically hissed aside as they approached.

News of the serial killer had hit hard Saturday evening. Lowell's father held a press conference to explain that there was a murderer in town, that he'd left behind clues in the form of letters on victims' cheeks, and why the community should be especially cautious the next day. He didn't mentioned Jill the Giant specifically, but insisted that there was "reason to believe" the killer might strike on Sunday. All the news stations and local Internet sites had flared with warnings of a killer stalking the town of Cowlmouth.

On Sunday, Cowlmouth was a ghost town. Douglas, like almost everyone else, stayed home all day. He spent the time playing video games and watching TV and instant messaging with Lowell and Audrey about the news.

There probably wasn't a dark window in all of Cowlmouth that night as residents stayed up late to hear if anything had happened. Douglas made it until about 1 A.M.

The next day, Douglas kept waiting to hear that some unlucky person had been found with an *S* carved into their cheek, just like Jill the Giant had prophesied. But it never came. Douglas wasn't sure what that meant.

He was sure, though, that he needed to know more about serial killers. More about murder. He needed to know why someone would chase a kid up the side of a house and carve letters into the faces of people. He needed to know why death could be unnatural. If all death was unnatural. If his family's business was a sham. If the entire business was based on pretending that everything about death was more okay than it was.

First, though, he needed to know more about serial killers. That's why he was dragging Lowell to the library.

Inside, Douglas felt the usual awe and confusion over its whispering paper innards. He didn't know how a library could keep track of so many books, even with those random-seeming numbers and letters taped to their spines. He was pretty sure that on past visits, he'd found entire catacombs of dusty tomes that hadn't been seen by library staff in years.

The pair passed by a large table near the entrance. It was always covered with books that were seasonally rotated. This month, the covers bore ominous houses and lurid monsters above names like Edgar Allan Poe, Ray Bradbury, Shirley Jackson, Washington Irving, Bram Stoker, and Edith Wharton. He flipped through a couple of the books and wondered whether any of the stories were about serial killers.

"Hey... isn't that the woman from Marvin's funeral?"

Douglas looked up to see the tall woman with glasses across the room, walking in their direction. She was wearing a long, blue dress covered with little brown starlings that looked like they were trying to fly away. Her head was turned to look down the rows of shelves, as if she was searching for something other than books.

"What? Is she following me?" Douglas ducked down a nearby aisle, with Lowell close behind. Douglas hid at the far end, while Lowell stood brazenly in the middle of the row, casually pulling a book off the shelf and perusing it. "Hmm . . . " He looked up and scanned the rest of the shelves. "Health and Medicine. Ever seen what a naked woman looks like?"

Douglas remained silent. He thought he could feel a cold wind as the woman passed by. "Can women be serial killers, do you think?" he asked the book spines in front of him.

After waiting a few minutes, Lowell poked his head out of the row, looked around, and motioned to Douglas. "Don't see her. Let's go."

"All right, but I really don't want to run into her again. Keep your eyes open."

They continued cautiously through the library like it was a museum full of exhibits untouchable behind glass. Soon they found themselves in the room full of computers. In this old building full of books, the two had headed right to the Internet to find answers.

The large chamber was lined with books on all four walls, and at its center were rows of long tables, each with two terminals. Between each computer was a brass lamp with a yellow shade and a printer with a sign taped to it listing the charges for printing.

Audrey was there, sitting at a table in the front corner. She was wearing a brown cardigan that caught her hair as it fell loosely to her shoulders. She was so engrossed in the screen that Douglas was half-tempted to sneak up and frighten her.

"Man, she beat us here. Your hearse needs a tune-up."

Douglas shrugged and dropped his backpack on the floor behind Audrey. She didn't turn around.

"Guys, look at this." She swiveled the screen a few degrees so that all three could see it. Douglas glanced nervously around the room before focusing his attention on the display, while Lowell grabbed an empty chair from the adjacent computer and sat down.

"What, you want ice cream?" asked Douglas.

"No, what are you . . . Oh." Audrey looked back at the screen and minimized the pop-up ad for Sweeney's Ice Cream Shoppe that had overtaken the page.

Framed in a mass of more advertisements below the header for the local paper, Douglas saw five words in a bold typeface large enough to be its own sound effect:

DAY KILLER PROWLS COWLMOUTH

"Day Killer?" asked Douglas.

"They've given him a name," said Audrey.

"Whoooooooa." Lowell elongated the syllable until his lungs ran out of air.

Douglas looked around and saw the computer screen one table over. It was displaying the same news story that they were looking at. An older woman in thick glasses, balancing an oversized white purse decorated in black cow spots on her lap, hunched in front of it. She bent over the purse until her face was only about an inch from the screen, an inch from the giant black letters that gave a name to the monster that was terrorizing Cowlmouth.

Douglas wondered how many of the people using computers in the room were reading this same news story and feeling the same horror, like stagnant water in their stomachs.

Douglas looked back at the screen and quickly scanned the article. Lowell's lips moved silently as he did the same. Other than the serial killer's nickname, it didn't tell him anything about the murders that they didn't already know.

"So everybody in Cowlmouth survived yesterday," said Lowell.

"Seems that way," Audrey said.

"Why are you guys talking like that's bad news?" asked Douglas, finally sitting down beside Audrey.

"It's great news, but . . ." Audrey pivoted in her seat and looked at Douglas. "It could come with its own bad news. I mean, we were all wrong about the pumpkin."

"Because nobody died? That just means the town took the warning seriously."

"Maybe. But I hardly believe that the . . . Day Killer . . . would've warned the town if he thought there was the slightest chance he could be stopped."

"Maybe it wasn't even him. Maybe it *was* a prank."

"And it's just a coincidence that the prank matched the signature evidence of the secret town serial killer?" Lowell asked. Douglas shrugged. But Audrey continued on.

"I'm sure the police are pursuing both those ideas. But they don't have the other thing."

"What other thing . . . Oh." His thing. Douglas Mortimer's thing. The being-chased-by-the killer thing.

"Right. If the *S* on the pumpkin didn't stand for Sunday and the Day Killer chased Doug on a day he already had a victim, then the calendar theory could be wrong."

Douglas smoothed the strands of hair angled across his forehead as the three sat in a silence broken only by the occasional library cough or click of a mouse. Audrey looked down at the keyboard, her finger trailing an invisible line between the *M* and *S* keys. She grabbed the mouse and selected a random link on the website. "So why are we here?"

"Man, I totally forgot about that," said Douglas. "I want to learn more about serial killers, even more after this conversation, and I don't want my parents to know that I'm researching this stuff." At home, it had taken a single grisly image popping up on the screen and almost being interrupted by his father to convince him that using his home computer for this type of research might not be in his best interests.

"So you're looking for privacy at a *public* library," said Lowell. "Got it."

Douglas scooted over to the other computer on the table and hit a key. The Cowlmouth Library mascot, a flying gargoyle with a book in its hands, froze briefly mid-flight before being replaced by the library Intranet Welcome screen. Douglas pulled the keyboard closer, called up a search engine, and paused before admitting, "I have no idea where to begin."

"Type in *murder*. That's how this whole thing started in the first place." Audrey looked around the book-lined walls until her gaze fell on the stairs at the back of the room. "You guys go ahead and look online. I'm going to see if I can find any books about serial killers."

Douglas watched her disappear up the stairs.

"Hope she doesn't get any paper cuts," said Lowell.

The library system had a content blocker on their network, but it wasn't too sensitive. He immediately realized, though, that he was at the wrong computer for calling up the horrible images of serial murder that slipped through the filter. Even with Lowell's gangly form at his shoulder, being at the front of the room made his screen visible to everybody behind him. He really needed his own laptop, he realized, putting it at the very top of the never-ending Christmas list in his head.

There were a lot of websites focused on serial killers. He could spend weeks looking through them all. He found lists of serial killers, most of them with violent and attention-grabbing nicknames just like the Day Killer. There were lengthy biographies of some of the more infamous ones, including pictures of their families and of them as children. He even stumbled onto crime scene photos, which he quickly closed after a quick peek.

He was so intent on his searching that when Lowell interrupted him with a "Hey, we done here yet?" Douglas jumped, his soul diving into the toes of his shoes. Lowell laughed loud enough to make the rest of the people in the room glance up from their computers. Douglas looked over at his friend—Lowell was playing a game on the adjacent computer.

"Yeah, I guess. Not making much progress." On Douglas's monitor was a map of the U.S. showing a disconcertingly consistent spread of serial killer activity over the past hundred years.

"I'm telling you, man. The only way to figure this whole thing out is to get out in the town. Walk the streets he walks. Creep in the shadows he creeps. Stalk the victims he stalks."

"Here comes Audrey," said Douglas.

"You guys find anything?"

"A little," replied Douglas. "Did you know that one of the first modern American serial killers was from New England?"

"H.H. Holmes."

"How'd you know?"

"Read it in this." She heaved a large book onto the computer desk with a thud that made the keyboard rattle. The title, *The Serial Killer Grimpendium*, was underlined by a knife and spelled out in big red letters that dripped blood. Below the knife was the subtitle *From Albert Fish to the Zodiac Killer* in similar bloody letters, with the whole arranged on a background of black-and-white mug shots, tiled like old yearbook photos.

"Cool," was Lowell's response.

To Douglas, the large, lurid book cover was almost as embarrassing as the questionable images on the Internet. "We should probably go look at this somewhere less . . . exposed."

"You afraid somebody's going to catch you reading an actual book?" asked Audrey.

"No. I'm worried about that woman over there." He pointed at a window in one of the doors at the front of the room, where he could see the head and shoulders of the tall woman he kept running into. She was talking to somebody on the other side and apparently about to enter. "Let's go to the Belfry."

The part of the steeple that once held the bell when the building was a church wasn't accessible to library patrons. However, people still referred to the large, third-floor room directly under the empty steeple as the Belfry. Foot-high, Styrofoam letters spray-painted gold spelled out the name above the entrance.

The Belfry was basically the reading room, with soft couches and upholstered chairs and large beanbags scattered around for people to sit in. A small counter in the corner carried snacks and drinks for sale at allowance-level prices, while shelves were arranged to divide the room into private nooks. Naturally, with Halloween only weeks away, the walls of the Belfry were covered with black construction paper bats.

The three friends picked out a couch in the corner that was hidden from the rest of the room by a pair of shelves. After a quick explanation to Audrey about the woman—quick because there wasn't much to say other than that she was spooky and always around—they sat down on the couch. Audrey found herself in the middle, so she took charge of flipping through the book. It was big enough that it covered her entire lap.

The inside of the book turned out to be more lurid than the cover. Every page had mug shots, victim pictures, crime scene photos, and images of evidence, the latter usually stained with dark splotches.

And the words were no less revolting.

People killed people throughout history, but it wasn't until the late 1800s when Jack the Ripper redefined the word *infamous* that the idea of an anonymous stalker-killer became a boogeyman in modern society. What Douglas found more interesting than the history, though, were the personalities of these murderers. Most serial killers hid their lives of crime behind everyday faces and everyday lives. They were neighbors, friends, parents, children, siblings. They held down jobs and went to church and shopped at grocery stores. Serial killers could be anybody. And yet, they were . . . different . . . broken . . . evil. He could see why his dad had such trouble talking to him about murder.

One quote caught Douglas's eye in particular. It was attributed to a woman whose daughter had been murdered by a serial killer. She spoke the words on the witness stand at the trial: "He's a monster." That simple. Without fang or claw or tentacle, the serial killer was a monster. That's what the Ghastlies had been calling the guy themselves.

The book was the most horrific thing Douglas had ever read in his life, and he was enjoying every minute of it. He was acutely aware of how close he was sitting next to Audrey, and hanging out there with her and his best friend made it almost seem okay that a monster was on the prowl in Cowlmouth. That death could be unnatural. *Almost.*

"Look at this." Audrey pointed with the hand adorned by the purple stone. "It says here that serial killers often choose their victims according to a pattern. The same gender, the same neighborhood, the same age, the same habits, the same physical description. That hasn't been true so far with the Day Killer."

"Maybe there's something the two victims have in common," Lowell suggested. "Where they lived or what store they shopped at, or something."

"If the killer's making a calendar, all he's looking for is a smooth cheek," said Douglas.

"So horrible," Audrey replied with a shudder. Douglas colored slightly. "Sorry."

"No, I meant what a horrible thing in general."

"Yeah."

"I know something they have in common," said Lowell. Audrey and Douglas waited. "The Mortimer Family Funeral Home."

"What?" asked Douglas.

"Just saying. Same morticians, same embalmer."

"Same reverend presiding over their services, same gravediggers putting them in their holes . . . same police officer in charge of investigating their deaths."

"Same kid sleeping above their corpses."

The trio should have laughed at the joke, but the reality of how close the monster was to their lives silenced them. Eventually, a tinkling intruded on their dark thoughts. After a bit of rummaging, Audrey pulled a phone from her backpack and answered it.

"Okay. I'll be right out." She pulled the phone away from her ear. "My mom. Gotta go. Let me know how the book ends." She stood up, grabbed her backpack, and was off around the shelf and down the stairs before either Douglas or Lowell could say goodbye.

Lowell took advantage of the extra space on the couch by stretching out his long form, laying his head back, and closing his eyes. Douglas nestled deeper into whatever room that left him, and flipped lazily through the remaining pages without really looking at them. He liked Audrey, but so far, all of their conversations were about serial killers. Can people build a friendship out of murder? It seemed an insane interest to share. Well, not an interest, maybe. More like a stake. Still . . .

An image on one of the pages caught his eye. It was a pen-and-ink illustration, heavy on the cross-hatching, of a dark figure. A white skull poked out of the hood of its bulky black robe. In one of its bony hands was a long, wooden staff topped by a curved blade. The figure dragged a limp body behind with its other hand. The caption read, "The Grim Reaper." In his mind, Douglas could see a bone-pale countenance framed in a thick black hood staring up at him from the bottom of a rope ladder. Cowlmouth's monster. The murderer. The serial killer. The Day Killer. He stared at the illustration for a good five minutes before slamming the book shut and smashing the robed skeleton between the pages.

Then he got up to call his mother for a ride home. As he stood, he realized that he had no clue where in the library Audrey had gotten the book from. He nudged Lowell, who was pretending to snore. "Do you have any idea where this book goes?"

"No. Does it matter?"

"I don't want to wander the library with this in my hands, trying to figure out where it needs to be re-shelved."

"You're Douglas Mortimer. People expect you to have something like that in your hands. Just leave it here."

Douglas didn't like that idea. A lifetime of putting away funeral programs and Mortimer Family Funeral Home pamphlets had made him a little obsessive about things being in their proper place. "Maybe I'll throw it on the Halloween table out front." If the staff didn't like it there, they could use their magic filing system to find the book's appropriate place.

He walked around the corner of the shelf . . . and almost ran into the tall woman in the glasses. She had been walking from the direction of the snack counter, and in her hand was a steaming paper cup with the unmistakably bitter smell of coffee wafting from it.

Startled, she looked at Douglas, and then down at the book in his hand. He looked down at it, too, surprised to see himself holding it like a dinner tray, the grisly red letters displayed as boldly as if they were written in neon-lit tubes. He tucked it quickly under his arm and nodded to her. "I know," he said. "Unwholesome."

He took off for the Belfry exit before she could reply, heading down the stairs. He could tell Lowell was following him from the barely stifled guffaws hitting the backs of his ears.

By the time Douglas got to the Halloween table, though, he had already forgotten about the woman in the glasses. All he could think about was the image of a skeleton in a black robe staring up at him from below his bedroom window.

OCTOBER 7

FRIDAY

CHAPTER 15

"What do you know about serial killers?"

Maybe it was a strange question for a boy to ask. Maybe not. It was certainly a strange question for a boy to ask a pair of dirt-covered men struggling to fit a gangly metal contraption around an open hole in the ground.

"This could do with a bit of oiling," Moss said to Feaster, trying to make the metal bars of the casket-lowering device telescope to the appropriate lengths. As usual, Moss was in a brown coat and slacks. Three watch chains dangled from pockets in his vest, none of which, Douglas knew, ended in watches. That was where Moss kept the keys to the graveyard's more expensive mausoleums. The ones filled with old, valuable statues and paintings. You can't take it with you, but you can stuff your tomb full of it. Moss's thick, black beard was flecked with dirt, and he'd stuffed his shapeless cap into his back pocket to let the cool air chill the sweat from his scalp.

Feaster, dressed in a green plaid coat and T-shirt bearing the faded image of a pair of moray eels, nodded his agreement as he struggled with the tubular framework. His long brown hair dangled free across his face.

Above, the sky was a somber gray that matched the gravestones surrounding them. It was the short mourning period of the day before the quickly falling October darkness blinked. Both men were trying to beat that blink so that everything would be ready for their scheduled graveside funeral first thing the next morning. Neither seemed to register Douglas's question. They kept huffing and grunting and sliding the sheathed parts of the framework in and out like some kind of large, experimental trombone.

Douglas helped as much as he could by arranging and adjusting the green mats of fake grass that covered the loose dirt that had been excavated. It was considered unsightly to have raw dirt exposed during a funeral. Piles of dirt were too close to the truth.

Today was Friday, and Douglas's mother had dropped him off at the graveyard right after school. He looked a bit ruffled as he adjusted the mats, his pants wrinkled at the backs of his knees and his red tie lolling out of his jacket like a thirsty tongue.

"Serial killers. They're monsters, right?" Lowell had said it. Audrey had said it. He had said it. The library book had said it. That had left Douglas only one place to go.

Feaster finally pushed the long hair out of his eyes and looked at Douglas. "That should probably be a father-son talk, Spadeful."

"We have talked."

"What did your dad say?"

"He said 'I don't know' a lot."

Moss took a heavy seat on the mat-covered pile of soil and scratched some of the dirt from his beard. "Wise man, your father. I've always thought that."

"It's death," Feaster agreed. "Being around so much death makes you healthy, wealthy, and wise."

"Minus the wealthy," finished Moss.

"Minus the wealthy," echoed Feaster.

"Well? The murderer's a monster, right? You won't be telling me anything I shouldn't know. Everybody at school is talking about the Day Killer. He's all over the news."

"He is, he is," agreed Moss.

"So?"

"Well, Spadeful," answered Moss as he settled his key chains, "you see, this type of monster, he doesn't really fall within our jurisdiction, you know."

"Jurisdiction?"

"He's not the kind of monster that we deal with. He's different."

"Why?"

"Well, first of all, because it's a *he*, and not an *it*."

"Could be a *she*," said Feaster with a hiss of satisfaction as a piece of the metal piping locked perfectly in place. "It's not unprecedented."

"Either way," explained Moss, "it's kind of a long story for a short autumn day, especially one that's about to drop *The End* here on us at any second."

"And we've got to get this here casket-dropper to install before it gets dark, else this whole project gets a lot harder to do." Feaster wasn't looking at Douglas when he said this, but at Moss, who was still casually perched on the pile of dirt.

"Yeah, that's right. Because of the gremlins." agreed Moss, not taking the hint.

"Gremlins?" Moss and Feaster barely needed to bait their hooks for Douglas to chomp down on them these days.

"Little mischievous beasties that only come out at night. They take pleasure in interfering with whatever it is you're trying to do. Make you have to work three times as hard to get something done or make it take twice as long. Fix a porch light? You'll lose your tools. Walk the dog? The leash will break, and your pooch'll run away. Grill a steak? It'll burn to a coal. And, whatever you do, never put up Christmas lights at night. Gremlins can really gum everything up. That's why most people work during the day and sleep during the night. Gremlins."

As tempting as it was, Douglas wouldn't be distracted by Moss's stories nor deterred by Feaster's impatience to get back to work. "Speaking of monsters, what can you tell me about the Grim Reaper? I mean, besides the obvious stuff."

Ever since he had seen that image in the library book, he couldn't get over how much it matched his impression of the Day Killer.

Feaster squinted at Douglas like he was out of focus. "Ha! Spadeful wants to know about the Grim Reaper."

"Death, himself, huh?" Moss heaved himself off the mound of dirt with some difficulty. "Now there's a serial killer for you. The worst of the lot. Also goes by Death Angel, Thanatos, Santa Muerte, the Black Mower . . ."

"I don't think he was ever called the Black Mower. You made that one up." Feaster chuckled under his breath. Douglas couldn't see what was so funny about serial killers. No one seemed to be as destroyed by the idea as he was.

"Allow me some license for my poetry, gravedigger. Besides if he hasn't been called that in all the millennia that he's been scouring the earth, he should be. In fact, the next time I see him, I'll dub him the 'Black Mower' myself." Moss delicately extended his shovel like a king knighting a kneeling man with a sword.

"The next time you see him, you'll have bigger concerns than nicknaming him." Feaster pushed back his hair, which seemed to prefer falling down the front of his face rather than the back of his head.

Moss turned back to Douglas. "I don't know if there's much to tell you that you don't already know. There's nothing too interesting about him. He's basically the postman, taking your box, so to speak, for delivery into the hereafter . . ."

"Here-under," interrupted Feaster, stamping a heel into the grave dirt.

"He's the narrator that gives the epilogue after the last chapter, the guy that rolls the final credits at the theater."

"You could even say he's your parents' best employee, what with all the business he drums up for them," added Feaster.

It was a joke, but the punch line horrified Douglas as he came to a disturbing realization: his parents were profiting off of the work of the Day Killer. Two funerals, two body preparations, two coffins, two plots, two burials, two headstones, flower arrangements, and publicity. That was a good bit of money. He tried to ignore the thought, but the shadow cast across his mind by the figure in the dark robe seemed to emphasize it all the more clearly.

"Why all these questions about serial killers and Grim Reapers?" Moss asked. "If I didn't know you had a fascination with death, I'd be worried that you had a fascination with death."

"Just curious. You guys talk a lot about monsters. You've never really talked about murderers."

Moss rolled his head back and forth on his neck, brushing his chest with his beard. "Maybe you should wait until you get a bit longer in the tie before you start trying to make sense of all this." When Douglas continued to stare stubbornly at him, Moss sighed. "Listen, you're talking about a different kind of monster. Not like a zombie or a mutant insect or a werewolf."

"So it's not a made-up monster."

"Whoa, whoa, Spadeful," Moss protested the statement by waving both his hands in front of him. "Monsters ain't 'made-up.' That's your mom talking. It's just that when it comes to serial killers, we call them monsters because it helps us come to terms with them. To set ourselves apart from them. As much as we can, anyway. We haven't quite figured them out, honestly, and by 'we,' I mean all of us adults. We call them monsters because their acts are monstrous, as monstrous as a blob from the depths of the ocean swallowing a swimmer or a succubus sucking the soul out of a sleeper. But they have a kinship with us—a kinship we don't like to admit, but a kinship nevertheless. They do monstrous things, but they're as human as your father or Reverend Ahlgrim. If you take the cells of a serial killer and the cells of an innocent newborn baby and stick them all under a microscope, you'll see no difference between them. Do you understand?"

Douglas kind of did to his surprise, but his mind kept returning to the vague dark form below his bedroom window. "I don't like this monster," said Douglas.

"That's good, Spadeful," said Moss. "Real good."

"Looks like your ride's here," said Feaster, nodding his head in the direction of the iron gates. Christopher stood on the far side of the black vertical bars, looking like he didn't want to come any nearer to them, their hole, or their coffin-lowering device. "Why won't he come on in?" asked Feaster. "He afraid we're going to ask for help?"

"Maybe he's not allowed on sanctified ground," said Moss.

"I don't know. Chris is being weird lately," admitted Douglas. "I guess I'd better go. You guys going to get this finished before night?" He looked up at the ashy sky doubtfully.

"Wouldn't be the first time we tended graves at night. It'll be romantic, just me and this old beard-hanger," joked Feaster, kicking a dirt clod at Moss.

"Well, watch out for gremlins," Douglas took off, leapfrogging tombstones to the gate.

At the gate, he didn't see a car. "Did you bring the hearse?" he asked Christopher.

"Nope. Walked." Christopher was in his work clothes, a black suit and a silver and gray-checkered tie, accented by a matching gold-plated tie clip and cuff links. His black hair was spiky with gel. They walked side by side down the walk, with Douglas taking two strides for every one of Christopher's steps.

"Did you have a removal today?"

"No. Been manning the storefront, waiting for sad people with dead bodies on their hands to come in and make pricey decisions."

"Why didn't you come into the cemetery?"

"Man, just because I have to sleep over the dead and wheel them around in boxes doesn't mean I want to traipse all over them when I can avoid it."

"You really don't like the dead. What'd they ever do to you?"

"You're a funny kid. It's all right for you. You grew up with dead people. They're like family to you. I'm in this because my pops thinks it's a good idea."

"That's why you took the apprenticeship?"

"Yeah. You can't get more stable than the death business. Always clients." Christopher looked around at the darkening shadows. "Especially with this Day Killer running around."

The row of dogwood trees was coming up, and Douglas made a point not to look too deeply past their trunks.

"I mean, nothing against your folks and all, but this death stuff . . . it's not me. I kind of knew that already, but I thought I could handle it. Work's not something everybody gets to enjoy. Now, though, with this Day Killer creep . . . I don't know if I can handle that kind of death."

Finally. Somebody who seemed as genuinely troubled by these murders as Douglas was. He should have talked to Christopher weeks ago. "I know. Suddenly death doesn't seem to be much of a life." Christopher nodded, stretching his upper lip with his top teeth until the sparse hairs of his moustache were parallel to the sidewalk. "What are you going to do?" Douglas asked.

"I don't know. Quit, maybe. That way, I can read about all this online like a civilized person who doesn't have to worry about death until they're old instead of having a murdered body two floors below the place where you're supposed to have sweet dreams."

The answer made Douglas's heart drop like it had only been thinly webbed into his chest. Chris might be feeling the same as him about the serial killer, but he also had an escape route if it got too bad. Douglas couldn't quit. Death wasn't his job; it was his family, his life.

He was stuck between a gravestone and a hard place.

The two walked in a heavy silence punctuated only by the leather soles of their dress shoes scraping the cement sidewalk. While they were still two blocks away, night fell completely.

In the dark, they saw the halo of pulsing red and blue lights before they saw the funeral home. Christopher was the one that acknowledged it first. "Not again."

CHAPTER 16

The funeral home was uncharacteristically lively, filled as it was with people who were all more vertical than the place was used to. Policemen, medical responders, and journalists were crowding the vestibule and front rooms of the house, talking excitedly and milling around the funeral home like they were at a party.

Christopher walked in dazedly while Douglas trailed behind like an afterthought. Douglas didn't see anybody he knew. They were probably all in the morgue fretting over the new murder victim with the new letter carved into his or her face.

What was today? Douglas thought. *Friday. An F, this time. A quick three slices for a sharp blade. Easy letter.*

Following Christopher through the rooms toward the back of the funeral home, they ran into a pair of police officers who had taken up posts on either side of the double doors that opened into the Hammond Mortimer Memorial Chapel. Douglas didn't recognized either officer. Things must be getting really bad if they were bringing in policemen from other towns to help. "You guys can't go in there," said one of the officers, quickly and authoritatively.

"I work here," answered Christopher as if hoping they would disbelieve him and send them away. "And this kid is a Mortimer."

"What are your names?"

"Chris. Chris Shin. And Douglas Mortimer."

"Okay. Go on in," The officer opened up one of the doors and shut it before they had barely crossed the threshold.

The chapel was empty, except for a solitary man. He was sitting on the front pew staring at the wall behind the lectern. As they came closer, he turned around and stood up wearily, settling into a posture that was slightly bent on top, like he'd hovered over too many sick beds.

"More murder?" asked Christopher.

"Officially, I can't answer that right now. Unofficially, I think I'm going to retire from being medical examiner. Stick to shining lights in people's ears and hitting their knees with rubber mallets." Dr. Coffman nodded at the youngest Mortimer. "Hello, Douglas. Nice tie."

Douglas absentmindedly brushed at a speck of grave dirt from the red fabric and asked, "Are my parents down there?" He inclined his head in the direction of the side door at the front of the chapel.

"Yes, they both are. They should be up soon, though. It's almost showtime. I'm up here going over my lines."

As he said this, the door opened, and Douglas's mother emerged from the storage room that led to the morgue. She looked harried, and one of her three necklaces was caught in her long red hair like it was a strand of spider web. "Oh, there you are, Chris. Could you go downstairs? They might need your help." Christopher winced, but obeyed.

Douglas's mother turned to him. "Douglas, you run upstairs to your room. You have company."

"Okay, Mom."

Dr. Coffman smiled at Douglas, reached into a pocket, and pulled out a disc of lemon candy without saying anything. Douglas took the offering automatically and left without a "What's happening?" or "What's the matter?" There was no need.

He made his way back to the front of the funeral home, through the crowd, and slowly ascended the stairs, as thoughts of a dark, fleshless figure haunted his imagination.

In his room, he found Lowell and Audrey sitting on the floor playing a video game. Lowell was a purple monster with bright red boxing gloves on each of its eight tentacles and Audrey was a furry silver creature with two sets of bat wings on its back and fists that ended in toothy mouths.

"What are you guys doing here?"

"Hold on. Give me two seconds to beat this loser . . . There!" Lowell exclaimed as the purple monster gave a rapid succession of uppercuts with each tentacle until the whole screen exploded in red and yellow. Audrey threw her controller down onto the carpet, and Lowell popped up from the floor. "We came over to plan our next steps for tracking down the Day Killer. Your mom said you'd be back soon, so we hung out in the kitchen with her for a while, but then everything started going crazy, so she told us to come in here and wait. If it hadn't been dark by that time, she probably would have sent us home."

"Yeah," agreed Audrey. "Plus, my dad's down there, Lowell's dad's down there, everybody's down there."

"Including another murder victim," Douglas finished.

"We eavesdropped at the top of the stairs for a while, but somebody busted us and sent us back here. It's definitely the Day Killer, and the victim is a man," said Lowell.

"Do you know who it is?"

"No, we didn't catch a name. We can find out later. But that's not the important question."

"What is?"

Audrey piped up. "We have to find out about the letter."

"*F* for Friday, right? *F* as in big fat failing grade. What does it matter?" asked Douglas.

"Because, if it's an *F*, maybe the Day Killer idea holds up," Audrey explained.

"In other words, *F* means it doesn't matter that I got chased."

"Don't put it that way, Doug," said Lowell. "It means that us keeping our mouths shut was the right decision. You don't always get that kind of confirmation in life, so you might as well jump on it when it comes around."

As soon as they said it, Douglas knew it was the truth. They had to find out if the Day Killer had left his mark, and what that mark was.

"So how are we going to find out?" asked Audrey.

"Well, I'm sure as hockey sticks not sneaking into the morgue again," said Lowell.

"You snuck into the morgue? That's crazy."

"Worse, it was at midnight."

"Invite me next time."

"Eddie will probably tell me," Douglas interrupted. "Or, heck, my father will probably tell me, now that these murders are out in the open. We'll have to wait until everything dies—settles down. I can message you guys later tonight."

"I don't think I can wait that long," muttered Audrey.

"Well, now that we've got nothing to do but wait, you up for a game? You're marginally better than Audrey." Lowell held up a controller as a shield while Audrey mock-punched him in the face.

"Nah," answered Douglas. "I think I'm going to hang out at the top of the stairs. See if I can hear anything. I have more practice doing it than you guys." He slipped off his shoes and soft-footed down the hall, keeping to the edges of the passageway until he reached the top of the stairs. He crouched to one side so that if anybody below got too close, he could be out of sight in seconds. From this vantage point he could see most of the vestibule area where all the officials and reporters were wandering around talking to each other and, like the Ghastlies upstairs, waiting for further developments.

A slight breath behind his ear made him realize that somebody had followed him. Assuming it was Lowell, Douglas almost threw an elbow behind him. Instead, he turned his head, and his face came within inches of Audrey's. She smiled tightly and directed her attention downstairs.

After about ten minutes of innocuous chatter, Douglas heard his father's unmistakable voice, but couldn't make out the words. Then Chief Pumphrey's voice boomed across the funeral home.

"We're going to have to ask all non-essential personnel to go home now. That includes reporters. Actually, that's aimed straight at reporters." A brief burst of argument was cut off when Chief Pumphrey continued. "We'll hold an official press conference tomorrow at the station. You guys have as much information as you need right now to go wild with all kinds of morbid rumors, so please—" An unintelligible drone of protest interrupted the chief.

The doorbell chimed to announce a new visitor, but the din from the reporters faded for only a second before returning to its protesting roar. Douglas craned his neck to see the front door. His father walked over and opened it. A woman stood on the front porch, a large canvas bag thrown over her shoulder. Douglas almost yelped when he recognized the tall woman. She really was following him around Cowlmouth.

"Mr. Mortimer?" she asked crisply.

"Yes, but I'm sorry, ma'am, we're closed right now. If you need immediate assistance, I can refer to you another funeral home close by."

"I'm not a client, sir. My name is Melinda Basford. This is my colleague, Diane Keeney." She motioned to someone behind her that Douglas couldn't see. "We're here to talk about your son, Douglas."

"Okay, but this is really, really a bad time. As you can see, we have quite a bit going on." He motioned to where the police chief and reporters were sparring behind him. "Please come back another time, and I'll be glad to talk to you."

"Understood. May we come back tomorrow?"

"Yes, yes, that'll be fine."

"Thank you, Mr. Mortimer." She turned around and disappeared from Douglas's line of sight. As his father closed the door, Douglas saw his mother join him.

"Who was that?"

"A couple of Douglas's teachers, I think. They're coming back tomorrow."

Douglas turned to Audrey behind him and shook his head while shrugging. He mouthed the words "not my teachers."

"Is anything wrong at school?" They heard Douglas's mother ask.

"I don't know. We didn't talk. They said they'd be back tomorrow. We've got plenty enough to worry about today."

"Mr. Mortimer?" Douglas could see Christopher now. "There's not much more I can do down there. I'm kind of in the way, honestly. Mind if I go up to my apartment?"

"Sure, no problem. You're on call tonight, right?"

"Yes, sir." Christopher exited through the front door. The entrance to his apartment was on the side of the funeral home, giving him some privacy and a flimsy way to segment his life from his work.

Douglas motioned to Audrey to follow him back to the room. Once there, he started putting his shoes back on.

"Where are you going?" asked Lowell, who was playing a video game by himself.

"Chris went to his apartment. He'll have the answers we need. You guys stay. I'll be right back."

"Nope. Coming," said Lowell.

"Me, too," said Audrey.

They followed Douglas down the hallway, through the kitchen, down the back stairs, and around the house to a side door. Behind this door was a set of steps that led above the chapel to Christopher's apartment. Douglas rang the bell.

A few moments later they heard the loud thumps of Christopher descending the staircase. He opened the door and popped his head out. A phone was pressed tightly against his ear, and he was speaking in animated Korean. He motioned for the three to follow him up. He had already taken off his jacket and tie, and his dress shirt was unbuttoned all the way to reveal a ribbed tank top underneath.

He opened the door and ushered them in, all the while speaking nonstop into the tiny piece of technology. The apartment was a studio with few pieces of furniture. A bed against the wall looked like it had never once been made, and a small, battered couch divided the room in two. A gigantic flat-screen television facing the couch was perched precariously on a pair of wooden barstools. Connected to the TV in about three octopi worth of wire tentacles was a DVD player, a cable box, and a video game system identical to the one in Douglas's room, although a cheap rack beside the TV showcased quadruple the number of games. On the walls were posters for movies Douglas didn't recognize, and scattered here and there were crumpled fast food bags.

Christopher finally lowered the phone and tossed it on the couch. "What do you guys want?"

"You were down there, right? In the morgue? You saw the murder victim?" Douglas was surprised to hear his questions come out more like demands.

Christopher sighed and rubbed vigorously at the sparse hair of his moustache. "Yeah, I saw him."

"Who was it?" asked Lowell.

"Some guy. Looked kind of old . . . forties, fifties, something like that. I didn't recognize him. A bus driver, I think."

"What about his face?" pressed Douglas. "Did he have a letter? What was it?"

"Man, I really hate this job." Christopher walked over to one of the crumpled fast food bags and rummaged around in it until he came up with a stale french fry. "Why in the world do you guys care?"

"Just curious," answered Lowell, his face a stone mask.

Christopher looked them over while chomping on the potato string. After he'd finished, he turned the bag upside down to see if there were any more survivors. "He had an *F* on his cheek."

"You saw it yourself?" asked Douglas.

"With my own two bloodshot eyes." He shuddered.

Douglas, Lowell, and Audrey looked each other in barely hid relief. "Good," mumbled Lowell.

"What?" Christopher shot him a look that was a muscle twitch away from him grabbing the boy by the collar.

"I said *good*," answered Lowell with a strange surge of confidence. "It means that this guy is following his pattern. That's extremely important if Dad and his officers have any chance of catching him." Douglas and Audrey nodded as if that was exactly what they had been thinking, too.

"I guess so. It certainly frees up everybody's Fridays," answered Christopher.

OCTOBER 8

SATURDAY

CHAPTER 17

What I wouldn't give for a sturdy coffin lid, thought Douglas, finally realizing why eternal rest mandated six feet of sunblock. He rolled over in his bed and pulled his blanket over his head to block the rays of late-morning sunlight that were infiltrating his window and burning the membranes of his eyelids.

Douglas didn't feel like getting out of bed. Didn't feel like getting dressed. Didn't feel like closing the blinds. Didn't feel like doing much of anything. He'd already ignored three texts from Lowell and one from Audrey. After they had learned which scarlet letter had been given to the murder victim, they decided to get together the following morning in the cemetery and figure out what to do. After all, the third murder victim had died on their watch, and the police now had three strikes against them. Everybody seemed at a dead end, especially the victims.

Based on how the murders had affected him so far, the fact that the Mortimer Family Funeral Home was hosting a third victim in its morgue should have made Douglas want to rip off his tie and run screaming from the house. However, at some point yesterday, whether it was seeing the mob of people in the funeral home or hearing Christopher's account of the dead man or even just waking up this morning angry at the sun, that terror had slipped down the emotional scale to apathy.

He looked at his alarm clock. The digits glowed a reproachful 10:00 A.M. His mother hadn't even come up to make sure he didn't sleep the day away. The murder victim was keeping her busy, he was sure.

Suddenly, he realized that his stomach didn't share his apathy. He wanted cereal. Douglas got out of bed and padded down the hallway toward the kitchen, still in the T-shirt and sweatpants he had slept in. As he passed the stairs, he heard the pleasant chimes of the front door downstairs. Another death, that's what those chimes usually meant. Someone else needing to put another ex-person into the ground. Another victim, regardless of the circumstances of the death. Murdered and mutilated or peacefully passing in sleep, just another victim of death, of the Grim Reaper.

Douglas really wanted that cereal.

He stopped at the top of the stairs and squatted down to give himself a better view of the front door. His father approached it. He was dressed in a black suit with a tranquilly patterned blue and green tie, and his black hair was combed with a precision that was the result of decades' worth of practice. He opened the door.

"Oh, hello . . ." His voice trailed off.

"Hi, Mr. Mortimer. I'm Melinda Basford. And this is my colleague, Diane Keeney."

"I remember."

The woman was back. Who on earth was she? Douglas could see her standing there in a maroon dress with flowers so tiny they might as well have been polka dots. Her brown hair was tightly curled and she wore thick-framed brown glasses. Over her shoulder was the same large canvas bag that she had brought yesterday. He couldn't see the other woman.

"I hope we didn't come too early."

"No, not at all," answered his father politely. "We're a twenty-four-hour service. Come on in." As the two women accepted the invitation, Douglas saw the one named Keeney. She was a black woman, much shorter than Ms. Basford and wearing a gray pantsuit with a ruffle-fronted burgundy shirt. He had never seen her before. "We can go into the sitting room," his father continued. "It'll probably be the most comfortable for us. Can I get you some coffee or something . . . ?" His father's voice trailed off as they walked deeper into the funeral home.

Douglas jumped up from his perch and ran back into his room. After rummaging through his closet for a few moments, he threw on a red robe, the one he had received for his birthday last year from his parents and hardly ever wore because, well, why would he? He was twelve years old.

He crept along the hallway and down the stairs and slunk his way to the entrance of the sitting room. As he approached, he heard his father say, "Sorry my wife couldn't be here. She had some business to attend to."

Douglas crouched with his back to the wall, right beside the entrance. Turning his head, he could see a corner of the room, the table with the golden Tutankhamun on it, and a bit of the cabinet of Mexican funerary figures.

"You and your wife are pretty busy right now."

"We usually are. We're a small operation. Of course, now, with the murders, it's a lot more hectic around here than usual, as you saw yesterday. So what exactly do you teach?"

"Teach? I'm sorry?"

"Aren't you Douglas's teachers?"

"No, no, we're not." The voice was light. It must have been the other woman, Ms. Keeney. "We're Guardian Angels."

"Guardian Angels. Mine?"

"It's a volunteer group here in Cowlmouth," answered Ms. Basford. "Like a neighborhood watch. Except that we watch out for local children. We're firm believers that it takes a village to raise a child. Or at least to keep them safe. It's a rough world out there. Especially in Cowlmouth these days."

"So you stake out playgrounds and bus stops? I have to admit, I am extremely confused right now," said Mr. Mortimer.

Douglas, sitting outside of the room on the hard floor, was also extremely confused.

"Let me see if I can explain," answered Ms. Basford. "I've been observing Douglas for the past few weeks now . . ."

"Observing him?"

"Nothing intrusive. Mainly, I've been coming to a few of your funerals, Irwin Stauffer's, Marvin Brinsfield's. Although I did run into Douglas at the library the other day by accident. I run a family support group there twice a week."

"I still don't understand. For what reasons are you *observing* him?"

"Well, Mr. Mortimer. We believe that Douglas might be in a somewhat unwholesome environment here."

"Here? You mean in his own home?"

"Exactly," answered Ms. Keeney. "Since his home is, after all, a funeral home, as well."

"Ladies, no offense, but I grew up here. My father grew up here."

"I understand that, Mr. Mortimer. But we live in different times. Much more complicated times. The wrong kind of influences can have far-reaching, negative effects on a child's life," said Ms. Basford.

Ms. Keeney spoke up, "Do you believe that being around all this death every day is healthy for a boy his age?"

"I do. Absolutely. Douglas is Exhibit A for that. He's one of the most well-adjusted kids you'll ever meet."

A footfall caused Douglas to almost take off running, but when he saw Eddie making his way across the funeral home, Douglas put a finger over his lips and bugged his eyes out in silent appeal. Eddie chuckled, shook his head, and kept walking.

"You must admit, at the very least, that it is a bit strange," pressed Ms. Basford. "I mean, right now, this second, there's a murder victim on the premises of this house."

"Directly below us, actually," corrected Mr. Mortimer. "And that's because there's a murderer on our streets. Can't much help that, you know."

"Right, and I realize the delicate position we are putting you in, and we appreciate that you haven't got defensive, but, well, at the library the other day, I saw him reading this." Douglas heard a soft scratching. He knew what the woman was drawing from her stiff canvas bag before he even heard his father read the title aloud.

"*The Serial Killer Grimpendium*, huh?" A few page ruffles later, Douglas heard his father add, "I can't blame him too much. News of this Day Killer is everywhere. It's healthy curiosity."

"Morbid curiosity," replied Ms. Basford.

"Sure, but that's a legitimate form of curiosity," countered Mr. Mortimer. "I'm sure most of the kids in Cowlmouth have the same questions, even the ones who aren't living in funeral homes."

"That's as may be, but for most of the children in Cowlmouth, these murders are a faraway thing, a story, something deep in the not-real space of televisions and computers. They don't have to face any of the victims. They don't have to sleep in the same house as them. They have natural buffers and harbors against the horrors of the world.

"Besides, for Douglas, it seems to be a bit of a tendency for him, even without the serial killer. He lives in a funeral home, plays in graveyards, wears suits all the time, spends his free time at funerals. Certainly you must see, if not a harmful pattern, at least a potentially harmful pattern."

"No, actually I don't." Douglas heard the slight shift of furniture legs against floor. "You know what I see? I see a boy who gets death better than most adults. I see a boy unafraid of it and channeling that strength into helping those who have lost loved ones. I see a mature, thoughtful boy with a genuine joy for life. One day, Douglas is going to run this funeral home, and he's going to be the best funeral director this old place has ever had.

"I mean, sure, right now, he might be a little confused. His entire life, we've taught him how much a part of life death is. We've probably over-sheltered him from the darker details, to be honest. But then the Day Killer strikes, and now he knows about it firsthand. It's a little too early for him to have to confront that, I think. And that's unfortunate. It confuses things for him. For all of us, actually." Mr. Mortimer paused. "So that we're clear, what exactly do you want to do about Douglas?"

"Well, we're not Social Services, obviously," said Ms. Keeney, "but we do have some relationships there and . . ."

"Relationships? I've buried the loved ones of some of the most powerful people in this town. People who know Douglas and would vouch for him."

While his father was speaking, Douglas had been staring with empty fascination at the golden statue of the boy king's sarcophagus. Tutankhamun had been nine years old when he became the pharaoh of Egypt, three years younger than Douglas was now. He had died nine years later, not even out of his teenage years. He must have dealt with a lot more in his short life than just a small-town serial killer. Or maybe running a kingdom was nothing compared to running from a serial killer.

"No, Mr. Mortimer," answered Ms. Basford. "I assure you, we don't want anything drastic to happen at all. We would just like permission to have some of our professional contacts observe him more closely. Interview his teachers and some of his friends. Perhaps get a psychological evaluation for him. And, in the interim, maybe you could shield him more, not allow him to attend so many funerals, for instance. We're only suggesting that you keep Douglas's childhood a little more distant from the more . . . unfortunate . . . aspects of your professional life. Nothing outrageous. And nothing that we don't think is in the very best interests of Douglas."

Suddenly, beyond the table and Tutankhamun statue, Douglas saw his father walk into view. He was facing the cabinet of Mexican funerary figures, studying them like they were far more interesting than what the Guardian Angels were saying. Mr. Mortimer must have seen his son out of the corner of his eye because he turned his head slightly from the clay sculptures toward Douglas's hiding place and arched one of his eyebrows high on his forehead.

Douglas got the message.

He jumped up quickly and quietly, tiptoed up the stairs to his room, and dived into bed. He grabbed a nearby plastic rose and strangled it by its stem in his clenched fist.

He was ecstatic. His father had said that he would be the best funeral director the Mortimer Family Funeral Home had ever had. Better than himself. Better than Grandpa. Better than Great-Grandpa.

But there was the other side of the conversation he had eavesdropped on, the side that damped his joy a little and made his stomach feel like it was full of the shards of broken urns. Those women said he shouldn't be growing up in a funeral home. Shouldn't be around so much death. He was certain that had his parents been anything other than morticians, he wouldn't be feeling what he felt now. Even Lowell and Audrey, as close as they were to everything that was happening because of who their parents were and, well, because they were friends of his, seemed better at dealing with the murders than he was.

Douglas didn't know what all was involved in a psychological evaluation, but if it made him feel better, he'd go through one. He thought about his grandpa for a while. Then he thought about the dead man in the dark, cold, metal drawer below and the *F* on his cheek. Monday, Saturday, and Friday. The monster wasn't even halfway through the week yet. This was a long way from over.

OCTOBER 15

SATURDAY

CHAPTER 18

Another night, another nightmare. This one was a confused mixture of chasing footsteps and thick fog and barely distinguishable whispering. It ended with a slow-motion race through Cowlmouth Cemetery, until finally, as the black bars of the gates emerged from the haze, Douglas felt his leg grabbed from below with a hand that felt cold, like dead bone, and he was shaken, shaken, shaken . . .

"Douglas, get up."

He slowly came out of sleep with a "Wuuth?" Blinking through the darkness, he could make out his father at the foot of the bed, his hand around one of Douglas's ankles.

"I need you to get up. We have a removal this morning, and I want you to come with me."

"I'm supposed to meet Lowell today."

"You'll have time later."

"Later? What time is it?"

"5 A.M."

"Wuuth?"

"Yes, Saturdays have 5 A.M's. Now, get up and throw a suit on."

Douglas obeyed. It wasn't until another twenty minutes had passed, after he had doused his head with water and thrown on a blue suit and a yellow tie with pale blue diamonds on it, that he realized where he was going. A removal. His father had never taken him on a removal before.

He grabbed his phone and sent the Ghastlies a quick message telling them that he wouldn't be able to go out until later. He wasn't quite sure what they were going to do. Probably patrol, maybe get some lunch, see a movie. It wasn't a Day Killer day, so they had free reign of the town.

The entire town of Cowlmouth had reset their calendars to this grim schedule. On days that the Day Killer had already claimed a victim, people let their guards down, let their children go to the playground, went to restaurants in the evening. On days that the murderer had not carved the corresponding initial into some unfortunate person's cheek, Cowlmouth became a ghost town, haunted by the slowly moving dark blue cars with the flashing lights on top of their roofs.

It had been more than a week since the last victim had been found. George Rivet had been his name, although everybody thought of him as the Friday victim. He had been a delivery driver, not a bus driver as Christopher had said. It was one of the many facts of George Rivet's life overshadowed by the last fact of his life, his murder.

Douglas met his father in the kitchen and followed him down the back stairs to the parking lot. It was still dark outside. The cold October sun couldn't be bothered kicking out from under its covers yet. As Douglas pulled himself up into the front passenger seat of the van, he could hear the metal clangs of his father checking the equipment in the back. Eventually, Mr. Mortimer slammed the back doors and jumped into the driver's seat. Before he'd even buckled his seat belt, Douglas started peppering him with questions.

"Where are we going?"

"We have to pick up a pair of bodies in Gorum."

"Where's that"

"About two and a half hours north."

"That's kind of far away for us."

"It's not our territory, but we're helping out Emmett's Funeral Home. They're really busy right now."

Even though we're the one with the murder victims. Douglas didn't dare speak the observation aloud.

Outside, dark houses were speeding past the window, each one shuttered against the horrors of the town.

"Why isn't Chris on this removal?"

"Chris quit two days ago."

"What?"

"Yeah. I wish he would have given a few weeks' notice, but the poor guy was definitely not cut out for this work. I kind of knew it when I hired him, but I needed somebody, and I thought I should at least give him a chance. He lasted longer than I expected."

After talking to Christopher on the way home from the cemetery last week, Douglas couldn't pretend to be surprised. But he was a little jealous. And he felt a little more alone. "The murderer," he said, not really meaning to say anything.

"Yeah. That put him over, I think. Want some breakfast?"

"Sure."

Mr. Mortimer pulled into the drive-through of the next fast food restaurant they saw. Food was one of the reasons that they took the van for removals. The black vehicle was unmarked and the windows in the back doors were tinted. Nothing about the vehicle would tip anybody off to its business, and that was a good thing when you had to run a quick errand or get some food. Nobody wanted to be creeped out by the knowledge that dead bodies were two parking spots away from them or at the drive-through window of their favorite burger joint. But sometimes you had to stop, whether you were carrying corpses or not. Of course, since there were two bodies to pick up this time, they needed the van anyway, which had a multiple-tray mechanism in the back that could hold up to three, stacked like they were in bunk beds.

As Douglas downed his orange juice and sausage biscuit, the sky began to lighten and his eyelids began to feel heavy. His father noticed. "Why don't you get some sleep? It's going to be a long trip."

Douglas nodded in acknowledgement and then in sleep, his head leaning against the cold glass of the window. He couldn't recline his seat because of the human trays in the back. Only the dead got to lay down in this van.

He slept well, until a loud ambulance siren startled him awake. It took a few groggy moments until he realized what the noise meant.

"Good morning, again," said his father.

"We're there?"

Mr. Mortimer only nodded since they were passing a large sign with the words St. Joseph's Hospital. The sign hung from a horizontal plank that was wide where it met the pole and thin at the far end and arced between the two in a gentle curve. *Like a scythe*, thought Douglas. The scythe-shaped posts were repeated throughout the hospital campus, each blade dangling friendly placards extolling hospital services along with images of smiling patients, doctors, and nurses. It seemed a strange motif for a hospital to adopt but, then again, few brains were as drenched by death as Douglas's to immediately recognize the vague similarity to the Grim Reaper's favorite walking stick.

The hospital was enormous, sprawling, and modern-looking. Its only real adornment was a large empty crucifix affixed to an otherwise blank brick wall of an upper story. They drove past its friendly signs until they reached the ugly back-end of the asymmetrical building. There were no windows on this portion of the hospital, only a line of large, retractable metal doors with white numbers stenciled above them. Mr. Mortimer slowed the van and consulted a yellow document that had been lying on top of the van's wide dashboard before driving the van toward one of the gray doors, putting the vehicle in reverse, and skillfully backing up until he was parked in front of it.

Mr. Mortimer turned off the engine and hopped out. Douglas followed. Taking in the sudden squalor of his surroundings, he figured it was an area of the hospital that patients never had to see. Well, unless they became un-patients, the type at the extreme bad end of the health scale. The area was filled with delivery trucks, large rusted green dumpsters, and, off to one side, a bunch of red bins labeled BIOHAZARD WASTE beneath branching six-pointed symbols. All under the shadow of a massive brown smokestack that towered into the sky.

Mr. Mortimer wasn't looking around like Douglas. Instead, he was studying a small panel to one side of the metal door. After a few moments hesitation, he hit a large orange button. A loud buzzing filled the air.

A few seconds later, the garage-style door started slowly rolling upward with a grumpy mechanical rumble.

Inside were about eight or ten cadavers on gurneys, each wrapped neatly in plastic as if they were fresh from a factory. They were positioned almost haphazardly, as if they had been pushed down a chute to end up at this loading bay.

Standing in the middle of all the tabled dead people like he was stuck to the hips in quicksand was a man. A big man. A huge man. He was completely bald and his lower lip was pierced by three gold rings. Two sparkly studs pressed into both sides of a nose that looked as if it had been pounded into his skull with a sledgehammer. A large black stone stretched his left earlobe, and his chin had about two days' worth of stubble. Both of his arms were covered in a confusing sleeve of sinuous tattoos. He wore bright pink scrubs.

The hulk spoke. "You here for the . . . Hey, is that your kid?"

Douglas's father nodded and drew Douglas closer to him. "It's a family business."

"Whatever, I guess. Bring your grandmother for all I care. Just glad you're here. Most of these bodies should have been picked up an hour ago. How many are you taking off my hands?"

"Two." Douglas and his father walked into the bay. It was cold and there were boxes of medical supplies everywhere, like a warehouse. "Here's the paperwork."

The big man took the sheets offered by Mr. Mortimer and glanced quickly at them. "You guys from Cowlmouth, huh? How's that Day Killer treating you? Getting much business out of it?"

"We've had better months," Mr. Mortimer responded neutrally.

"Whatever, I guess." The pink giant lumbered over to a small station covered in similar sheets. "Let me fill this out," he growled. "You'll have to look around. I'm not sure which of these guys are yours."

"Not a problem," Mr. Mortimer answered. "Douglas, do me a favor and go unload the gurney."

"Okay, Dad."

Douglas walked to the back of the van, opened it, and struggled with the collapsible metal contraption for a few minutes. Finally, he was able to pull it out and unfold the legs.

By the time he pushed it up the ramp and into the bay, his father had already found one of the bodies and was busily checking it for personal effects and double-checking the hospital bracelet to ensure it was the correct body. Mistakes were made at every kind of job, but morticians didn't get any allowances for theirs.

While his father picked over the carcass, Douglas looked around. He had never been on a removal before, and he was fascinated. This was a part of the business he had wanted to experience for as long as he could remember.

"Okay, Douglas. These two are ours." Mr. Mortimer handed Douglas two bags full of the personal effects. Naked come we into this world, and covered in jewelry, phones, and keys shall we return, as Eddie liked to joke. "Hold these while this gentleman and I load Mr. Carnegie and Mrs. Dallas into the van." The attendant scowled and scratched at the naked dome of his head, but didn't say a word as he helped Douglas's father with the bodies.

With Mr. Mortimer at its shoulders and the big man at its feet, they heaved one of the cadavers off its gurney on the count of three, and laid it as gently as they could onto the empty gurney from the van. They rolled it the short distance to the back of the vehicle and loaded it, afterward repeating the process with the second one. After a few signatures were exchanged and Mr. Mortimer picked up a receipt for the transaction, he and Douglas got back into the van for the long trip home. It was only nine in the morning.

"Well, what'd you think?" Mr. Mortimer asked after they had left the grounds of the hospital.

"It was kind of boring."

"Yup. That about sums up this kind of removal. Just your basic transaction. Lots of paperwork. Lots of people detached from what it is they're transacting. Now, if this had been a home removal, it would have been a totally different experience. When we have to pick up somebody from their own house and from their own family, well, it can be the most heartbreaking part of the whole funeral process."

After about ten minutes of driving in silence, Mr. Mortimer spoke again. "We ready to talk about last Saturday?"

"Those women who came by?"

"Yes. The Guardian Angels. Of all the silly . . . Well, I shouldn't say that. They're well-meaning. Just nosy. But sorry I haven't been able to talk to you about it yet. Been so busy. I'm always pretty busy, huh?"

"It's okay."

"Did you eavesdrop long enough to get what they were saying?"

"They didn't think that it was . . . wholesome . . . for me to grow up in a funeral home."

"Yes, they didn't seem to. What do you think?"

"I don't know. Before the murders, I would have thought they were crazy. Now? I think I understand why Chris left."

Mr. Mortimer sighed. "The mortician's life is tough, whether you're a grown-up or a kid, but especially if you're a kid. You know so many things about death that most kids don't have to know for many, many years, if ever. I mean, there are dead bodies a few inches behind you right now, for goodness' sake. Most kids don't come within miles of it growing up. Maybe they have to go to the funeral of a grandparent, but seeing a family member in the box of honor at a funeral is completely different from picking up a strange body from a hospital.

"On top of that, after you've learned that death is as much a part of life as living, you're given a lesson even you shouldn't have to learn for a long, long time. . .

That it's a bit more complicated than merely being a part of life. That it's not all loss and comfort and moving on. That sometimes, it's terrifying, disgusting, discomforting."

"Why do we do it? The funeral home business, I mean."

"Well, partly because that's all we've known. My father raised me this way, like his father raised him. Like I'm raising you. But also because we get real satisfaction from helping people." Mr. Mortimer paused, running a finger over the top of the steering wheel. "Honestly, though, it's mostly because we can."

"We can?"

"Not everybody can deal with the dead on a regular basis. Chris couldn't, and he's not a rare case. It's not even a fault that he can't deal with death. It just is. He can't. I can. Sky is blue, grass is green, and the sun is extremely bright." Mr. Mortimer lowered his visor.

Douglas drew invisible letters on the window, concentrating on not looking at his father. "What if I can't?"

"That is a definite possibility. Heck, my brother couldn't. First chance he got, he jumped into a different business. He'd rather get his clothes all dirty landscaping a yard than wearing a tie and rolling a coffin around."

"When will I know?"

"I don't know. Not yet, I don't think." His father hit a button and adjusted the side view mirror. "But I'll tell you this . . . You're pretty amazing with it, considering how old you are. When I was your age, I only attended a funeral or visited the graveyard when my parents made me. The family business was the furthest thing from what I wanted to do on any given day. But you . . . Honestly, it wouldn't surprise me if you took this whole thing over and made the Mortimer Family Funeral Home the biggest success it's ever been."

"Is that why you're letting me come on this removal?"

"Sort of. You'll need the experience eventually, but between you, me, and our two trustworthy passengers back there, I need the help right now, what with Chris gone."

Douglas sat back in the seat and thought for a second. "Dad?"

"Yes?"

"I don't have to if I don't want to, right?"

"Don't have to what?"

"Take over the funeral business."

"No, of course not. But this is a conversation I should be having with an eighteen-year-old Douglas. Maybe even a twenty-five-year-old Douglas. Right now, we should be talking about your schoolwork, your friends, your favorite YouTube shows. You have a girlfriend yet?"

Douglas ignored the question. "I don't know enough about death to take over the funeral home."

"Sure you do. You don't need to know much. I didn't when I started, and I don't even know that much now. Besides, it's the living you need to become an expert at. I mean, sure, we serve both the living and the dead. But, between the two, the living are the more important. They're the ones who pay the bills." Douglas's father grinned and elbowed Douglas across the center console.

Douglas smiled. "So the Guardian Angels, they're wrong?"

"Douglas, I've never met two more wrong people in my life. Nice people, don't misunderstand me, just unqualified brain donors when it comes to understanding the Mortimers."

"So it's okay if . . . if I'm curious about the Day Killer?"

"To a point, yes."

"What point?"

"I don't know. How about I let you know when you get there?"

Douglas pushed on, encouraged by what his father was saying. "You saw the latest victim's face, right?"

Mr. Mortimer paused for a second, a strange hesitation from a man whom not an hour before walked his son into a bay filled with dead bodies. "I did," he finally answered.

"You saw the letter. The *F*? There was an *F* on the corpse's face?"

"Mr. Rivet?" As a general rule, Douglas's father didn't like referring to the deceased like they were objects. He always called them by their names. "There was."

"And an *M* on Mrs. Laurent and an *S* on Marvin?"

"Yes, I saw them all. Why do you ask?

"Seems important to hear it from you instead of the news or rumors at school."

"The whole thing is real. Too real. Or just real, I guess, no 'too' about it." His father's tone slipped into the subdued, and it seemed he was watching the road in front of them in a completely different way. Douglas decided not to disturb him, instead leaning his head against the window and letting the vibrations travel through his skull to tickle the skin of his nose. His father was the one who broke the silence.

"You want to know a secret?" It was the only question in the history of the human race that has never received a "no." Douglas nodded. "I wasn't always okay with death."

"Really?"

"When I was in my twenties, I had to help my father deal with a pair of young parents who had lost their daughter. Had to help him with the removal, a home one. I'll never forget her name . . . Candice. The worst part was that she choked to death. On a radish. A stupid little radish. I almost gave it all up."

"But you didn't."

"No. I gave up radishes for a time, though. The thing is, no matter how hard it was for me, it was a thousand times harder for her parents, for her grandparents, her aunts, her uncles, her cousins, the friends of her family. I finally realized I was being selfish. These people needed help, and we were the ones that could help them."

"So I'm being selfish?"

"No, no. Man, I'm really bad at this. We're going to have to have another child so I can get a do over. You see, I was in my twenties. You're just a kid. Besides, you have to face this doubt at some point. Better now than later, but you can do it both now and later, too. Might be better that way." Mr. Mortimer took his eyes briefly off the road and looked at Douglas. "You know what, though? You can take it. Like I said, you're pretty amazing at this." He cocked his head back toward their cargo, somehow making the two bodies symbolic of the whole fate of humankind in doing so.

Douglas didn't feel amazing, but he did feel better.

CHAPTER 19

For more than a month, the town of Cowlmouth had been spooky for all the wrong reasons. Today, as Douglas looked down Main Street, it was spooky for all the right ones.

Along the street, every lamppost flew a faded black banner with white puffy ghosts floating above the words HAPPY HALLOWEEN in shivering yellow letters. Cowlmouth had hung those banners every year that Douglas could remember. Shop windows glistened with gels of orange pumpkins and black cats or were painted with pointy-hatted witches and decapitated skulls with smiles friendlier than any pair of lips could achieve.

Douglas stood outside the window of Sweeney's Ice Cream Shoppe. It would be closing for winter in a few weeks, but today it was ready for Halloween. Inside the front display window wafted helium balloon ghosts covered in white sheets with black construction paper eyes. A small chalkboard on an easel advertised pumpkin-flavored "Eye Scream" in letters drawn out of green pumpkin vines.

After he and his father had returned home from the removal, Douglas helped transfer the bodies to the morgue and then excused himself after he found a message from Lowell telling him to meet at Sweeney's. Douglas was ten minutes early, but he had enough time to take in the Halloween surroundings because none of the other Ghastlies seemed to be there yet.

In fact, it looked like they were the only ones in town who weren't around. Since it was a Saturday—a day that the Day Killer had already crossed off of his morbid calendar—a respectable number of people walked the decorated street. Inside Sweeney's, a long line snaked to the ice cream counter despite the cool temperatures outside. Actually, Douglas realized, he wouldn't mind a hot caramel sundae.

He had just started checking his pockets for money when, on the edge of his vision, he registered a strange hopping motion. Turning his head, he noticed a small white sphere, no bigger than a dandelion puff, jumping in long arcs against the sidewalk until it hit the side of the building and settled into a crevice. Douglas brushed at the hair on his forehead and walked over to pick it up. It was a human eyeball. Or, at least a small rubber ball painted to look like one. Red veins spider-webbed across the surface and a black pupil stared blindly up at him from the palm of his hand. The iris was a monstrous yellow shot through with green streaks. So maybe not exactly human. He looked around to see if he could figure out its source and saw another hopping motion. Another eyeball. He chased it down and picked it up. This one had a red iris. Neither seemed to come from anywhere.

As he stood there with an eyeball in each hand, his own eyeballs rotating in confusion as he tried to figure out what was happening, he felt light impacts on his shoulders and head. More eyeballs were bouncing off him like gentle hailstones. Before he could look up, a deluge of rubber white eyeballs with yellow, green, and red irises cascaded down, rebounding off him and bouncing on the sidewalk and road like the eggs of a confused flock of birds.

As quickly as the eyeball storm started, it stopped and, with the exception of a few overly energetic orbs that caught a lucky slope and careened down the street, eventually settled. Douglas could see people all down the street had stopped to stare at him. He looked up, both to avoid their gazes and to see where the eyeballs had come from. Against the sun, he saw a spindly, familiar silhouette accompanied by a second, shorter one peering over the edge of the roof.

"There's a ladder around back," said the spindly figure.

Douglas found the iron rungs bolted to the back of the one-story building. After a brief hesitation made up of one part feeling ridiculous for climbing onto the roof of an ice cream shop and one part terrifying flashback to the last time he had climbed a ladder, he ascended to the roof where he found Lowell and Audrey waiting. They weren't even trying to control their laughter. Lowell was holding an empty plastic bucket with a garish label that read MONSTER EYES.

"Why?" was all Douglas said.

"The eyeballs were my idea," piped in Lowell between

guffaws. "Found 'em in the Halloween section of the dollar store down the street. As for the roof, I wish I could take credit for that one. That's all Audrey."

Douglas turned to her expectantly. She answered, "It has nothing to do with dropping eyeballs on you."

"Yeah, it has to do with the monster," said Lowell excitedly. "Tell him, Audrey."

"Well, I overheard something my dad was telling my mom . . ."

"Down a staircase?" asked Douglas.

"No, and not through a vent, either. We were all just watching TV, and I guess they thought I wasn't paying attention to them. He said that because of the Day Killer, they've started new procedures at his ambulance service for what to do on crime scenes. That got me to thinking about the crime scenes themselves, that we should check them out if we can."

"See, told you having the daughter of an ambulance driver would come in handy. If only she were better at video games."

Douglas waited a few seconds for Audrey to continue until he realized that she was at the end of her explanation. "So how does the roof of an ice cream shop fit into this story?"

"Oh. This"—Audrey raised her arms and half turned—"is one of the crime scenes."

"Sweeney's?"

"No," said Lowell. "Sweeney's roof."

"What?"

"This is where they found Mrs. Laurent."

"Are you sure?" Douglas looked around. The roof was flat and had a one-foot-high wall surrounding it. Slits were cut into its base to let rainwater escape. In the middle of the roof was a large, square ventilation system, and a few pipe-like protrusions the purpose of which Douglas couldn't even hazard a guess at, sprung up here and there.

"Yeah," answered Audrey. "After what my dad said, I went online and found a whole website about the Day Killer that listed all the crime scenes. I was able to cross-check them with articles from the local news."

"Get this, though," said Lowell. He'd slid his phone out of his pocket and was taking pictures of the roof-top like it would disappear at any moment. "The site was from a guy in Montana. Montana! The Day Killer is making Cowlmouth famous."

"Infamous," said Audrey. "Some places are even calling him the Cowlmouth Killer. Points for alliteration."

"But, man, oh man, is there more," said Lowell. "There's a bloodstain." He pointed at a dark splotch on the inside wall at the front of the roof.

"We think it's a bloodstain, at least," said Audrey.

Douglas crouched down to look closely at it. The dark splotch was brownish and shaped a little bit like New Hampshire. It did look like dried blood. Douglas had seen enough of it on Eddie's aprons. "So this is where Mr. Laurent would have been."

"Yeah, I mean, think about it. The killer was up here. Right where we're standing," said Lowell.

"Killing someone," Audrey finished soberly.

"Or placing her here after killing her somewhere else," observed Douglas.

"No less grisly," said Audrey.

"Still . . . on the roof? That makes no sense." said Douglas.

"He's a monster. He has his own ideas of sense," replied Lowell, who had found an interesting angle on the stain and was celebrating by taking a dozen pictures of it. "But it actually does make sense. He's not trying to hide the bodies. He's carving messages into their faces. Messages are meant to be read, remember? He set Mrs. Laurent here on the roof and lowered her arm down so that anybody walking past the shop would see it. Can you imagine that? On your way over for a banana split and you see a dead hand dangling up there like a fishing line." Lowell mimed holding one of his hands limply in the air with the other.

"Where were the other victims found, hanging from the water tower? Lying in the arms of the founder's statue at Town Hall?"

"Marvin was found in a vacant lot beside Hiram's," explained Audrey. "It's one of the most popular restaurants in town. Mr. Rivets was found on the side of the highway . . . propped up in the driver's seat of his delivery truck."

"Who knows how many people drove past him thinking he was taking a break," added Lowell.

"We'd need a car to get to the other two spots, but this one was close, especially to your place, Douglas. Which is probably one of the reasons that your funeral home got tapped to take the first victim instead of one of the other funeral homes in town. And I guess you got the rest because you got the first."

"Lucky us," said Douglas. He walked over to the edge of the roof and gazed down Main Street. "I wonder how far across town you could get just by using the roofs?"

"I don't know, but now that we're up here, I kind of want to figure out a way to get to the other murder scenes," mused Lowell. "Maybe we can convince Chris or Eddie to take us?"

"Chris quit. Eddie might, I don't know."

"Chris quit? I always thought that guy hated dead people. We should at least do more than fill Doug in on everything that he's missed by not hanging out with us enough." He threw Douglas a mock-stern look. "We should look around a little. See if there are any more bloodstains."

It almost took less time to search the roof than it did for Lowell to suggest it. All they found was a sealed can of paint and a fist-sized hunk of concrete that somebody must have thrown up there. They didn't find anything by peering down into the alleyways that surrounded the shop either.

The three Ghastlies settled beside the large vent. Lowell picked up a stray eyeball and bounced it on the roof.

"Are you okay?" Audrey quietly asked Douglas. "You seem far away."

"Well, I'm twelve years old, sitting at a murder scene, trying to find a monster whose victims keep ending up in my house. Oh, and who might have chased me outside my bedroom. And slashed a giant pumpkin while I stood oblivious nearby. I kind of would like to be far away."

"That surprises me."

Douglas looked over at her. "What?"

"You're Douglas Mortimer. The Cadaver Kid."

"The Cadaver Kid. Haven't heard that one."

Lowell laughed. "Me, either. It's a good one, though."

"You're the boy who gets death. While the rest of us don't know a thing about it, you've already seen it, dealt with it, and moved on. You're way ahead of us."

"You two seem to be much better at handling this whole serial killer business than I've been. I haven't seen Lowell this excited in a long time, and you're all making plans about finding him while I'm moping in my room."

"Come on, man," said Lowell. "You're closer to this than the rest of us. You were the one that had the encounter, and you are the one who has the reminders of the deaths in your basement. You have no place to hide from it. Of course it's going to be different for you."

"He's right. But that's not even what I'm talking about," said Audrey. "You seem to get this whole thing better than us, deeper than us. We're just playing a game. We know we're not going to find anything at this crime scene, that wandering around town is hardly patrolling, that midnight meetings in cemeteries are completely unnecessary. We're having fun."

"Isn't that a healthier place to be? I've heard that being around too much death is a bad thing for kids our age. We're not supposed to know anything about it. It's supposed to be a game." He loosed his yellow tie down his chest with a quick pull at the knot.

"My father shields me from a lot of his work," said Audrey.

"He does?"

"Since he's a first responder, he sees a lot of bad stuff. Car wrecks, construction site accidents. I guess he can add murder scenes to his résumé, now." She paused and ran her hand through her hair a couple of times, the purple stone surfacing here and there from its black depths like an exotic fish. "All types of gruesome stuff that he won't tell me a thing about."

"Same here," said Lowell. "Dad still thinks I believe he runs around blowing a whistle at bank robbers in eye masks, like in the cartoons."

"So?"

Audrey looked down at her hand and twisted her ring, the purple stone disappearing and reappearing with each revolution around her finger. "I wish my dad would tell me more. At least some of it. Like your parents let you in on stuff. I feel like a big part of the world and a big part of my father is hidden from me. A part of the world I need to know about if I'm ever going to make sense of it. And it's a part of my father I need to hear about if I'm ever going to really know him."

"I'm sure your dads will tell you more eventually."

"Right. When I'm old enough. That's what he says, too. Have your parents ever told you that?"

Douglas tugged at the strands of hair on his forehead and thought about it. "They don't always let me in the morgue when Eddie's working."

"But you know what he's doing down there. Maybe my father's right. Maybe I'm not ready. Your parents seem to think you are. That says something."

Douglas didn't respond immediately. Finally he said, "I like your ring."

"Thanks." Audrey held it up higher in the late afternoon light. "The stone is amethyst. My aunt got it for me when she visited London last year. I like your tie."

"Don't get him started," said Lowell. "Next thing you

know, he'll be listing all the knots he knows." He raised his voice half an octave, "Windsor, Half-Windsor, Pratt, Four-in-Hand . . ."

"You know all those knots?"

"My parents taught me by letting me tie the ties on the deceased for funerals. Then I started tying my own ties. I used to wear clip-ons, but people at school kept yanking them off. Like this guy over here." He elbowed Lowell in the ribs. "Let's go down and get hot caramel sundaes."

"Audrey," said Lowell as they made their way to the ladder at the back of the building. "Have I ever told you about the time me and Doug snuck into the crematorium? It's a great story."

Douglas didn't immediately follow them. It wasn't that great a story. He walked to the front corner of the roof, purposefully avoiding looking at the dark stain just a few feet away. The sky was as colorless as bone ash, and a slight autumn breeze chilled his cheeks. From here, he could see all the way down the street and over the rooftops of the shops across the way. It was the center of Cowlmouth. Infamous for its Day Killer. And that fiend was out there somewhere, counting the days.

The ghosts on the lamps poles flickered here and there in the breeze.

OCTOBER 31

MONDAY

HALLOWEEN

CHAPTER 20

The paper tombstones on the back of their chairs were ripped where they weren't torn down. The inflatable Frankenstein's monster had lost a quarter of its air, causing its square head to cant to one side like it had broken its neck. And there was a large box of turkeys and Pilgrims sitting on the desk where the jack-o'-lantern had been, itching in their feathers and black wool for their turn at Miss Farwell's classroom.

It was Halloween. You could feel it. Halloween always felt different.

And this Halloween felt even more different.

Partly, because Cowlmouth had an actual monster

on this holiday of monsters. Mostly, though, it was for another reason.

It had been more than three weeks since George Rivets had been found behind the wheel of his delivery truck. More than three weeks since the last murder. Three weeks ago, the biggest decision that had to be made was whether to leave the house. Today, it was whether to cancel trick-or-treating.

It would be the first Halloween in the history of Halloweens to not have trick-or-treating. One could make the case that it wouldn't even be Halloween without trick-or-treating, and, in fact, child philosophers all over Cowlmouth were making such a case.

For the coffee-drinkers, it wasn't an easy decision. After all, at some point the town had to return to business as usual. That point might as well be Halloween.

So for the entire week leading up to the holiday, the students had been wondering whether they would be allowed to haunt the houses of Cowlmouth, moaning doorbells and rapping doors like ghosts at a séance. Whether the costumes that each one had bought or created would get any use, or whether they would have to be packed away for another year, empty monsters in boxes, tucked away in closets and attics and under beds.

It was after lunch when Miss Farwell finally made the announcement. "I know you're all waiting to hear if trick-or-treating will be canceled tonight." She paused and her hand played with one of the flaps on the cardboard box of Thanksgiving on her desk. The sixth graders' anticipation expressed itself in a level of quiet that might have rivaled the Mortimer Family Funeral Home morgue at its deadest. "Well, the school board and the mayor and the police chief have all met." She paused again, and Douglas could almost hear her planning the recipes for Thanksgiving dinner in her head. "And because today is a Monday and because it's been three weeks since anything . . . bad . . . has happened, they've decided not to cancel trick-or-treating."

The uneasiness broke in a wild cheer that almost left a few of the students too hoarse to even say "trick-or-treat." Douglas joined in, despite being all too aware of the sad reason why they were going to be allowed to put on costumes and hunt for candy door-to-door. *Thanks for taking Monday for us, Mrs. Laurent.*

"Hold on, quiet down, quiet down." The students settled back into their desks, visions of tiny candy bars and gummy insects dancing in their heads. "There are some rules that will be imposed to ensure your safety.

First, there's a curfew. Nobody under the age of eighteen may be out past eight o'clock."

The musical scale doesn't have an *aw* note among its *do*s, *re*s, and *mi*s, but Miss Farwell's audience was able to collectively find one to hit so perfectly it would have made their music teacher proud. Halloween was the one night reserved for kids, the one night they didn't have to come home when the streetlights came on, and the one night when being a school night didn't matter.

"Stop it. That gives you plenty of time to trick-or-treat. Second, if you're not going with your parents or other adults, you must be in groups of at least three. The police are increasing their patrol tonight as a safety precaution, but if any of them see a group of fewer than three trick-or-treaters, no matter how old those trick-or-treaters may be, the officer will pick them up and escort them straight home."

"I'd rather see what it's like to ride in a cop car than beg for candy, anyway," Douglas overheard somebody whisper from the back row.

Douglas was happy that Halloween wasn't canceled, but it was an emotion that had a lot to compete with inside of him. He leaned back in his chair, his thoughts less focused on the costume that was currently waiting for him on his bed, and more on murder. Three weeks wasn't enough to make him forget it, even a little bit.

Currently, he was thinking that if it weren't for the murderer, they wouldn't need to be in groups of at least three. And also if it weren't for the murderer, he wouldn't have two friends to go trick-or-treating with. Lowell would have been around, of course, but Douglas probably wouldn't have met Audrey. That was something. Maybe it was salvage in this situation, but it was still something.

The high-pitched scrape of chalk on the board broke his reverie, making him realize that Miss Farwell had moved on from this year's Halloween rules to those of English grammar. He opened his textbook and tried to concentrate.

Of course, now that trick-or-treating was officially on, the rest of the day dragged like a corpse without a gurney. Eventually, the final bell rang, and Douglas took off to climb into his waiting hearse to head for home.

In his room, Douglas sat at his desk and stared at his costume. It was laid out flat on his green comforter and looked like somebody had disappeared in their sleep, leaving only empty clothes behind. With everything going on over the past month and a half, he hadn't thought too much about his costume, but when it was time to choose one, it was obvious what he would be.

Most coffee-drinkers thought Halloween was about fantasy. That's why they encouraged kids to dress up as princesses and warriors and superheroes. But that wasn't the truth. Not really. Any day could be, and was, about fantasy. Just because a five-year-old was only allowed to put on a princess getup in public once a year, didn't mean the child wasn't pretending to be one on the other 364 days. No, dressing up on Halloween was never about the fantastical; it was about fears.

Moss and Feaster, who claimed to face the town's monsters nightly, had always told Douglas that Halloween was the one night of the year when everybody else could face down monsters, too. On Halloween, people didn't need to be afraid of what they were afraid of every other night on the calendar. Creatures in closets. Things that go bump in the night. Scaly hands reaching from under beds. Shadows across ceilings. Voices gurgling in the plumbing. Dark, hungry basements. Death. Well, they were afraid of them, but not in the same way they usually were. Maybe that's why the town was okay with having Halloween despite the Day Killer. Sure, they had other reasons to allow it, but when it came right down to it, maybe Halloween was the one day that Cowlmouth could finally face its monster.

To face his own monsters, Douglas had chosen an oversized hooded black robe, an undersized plastic scythe, and a flimsy skull mask that affixed to his head with a thin elastic band. Douglas Mortimer, Grim Reaper. He was in charge of his own soul tonight.

"You sure I can't paint your face, Douglas?" mumbled Mr. Mortimer as he stood in the doorway, an orange bowl of candy corn in his hand, a handful in his mouth. Both his parents had wanted to paint his face to look like a skull instead of buying him a mask. But not because they minded spending a few bucks. Being morticians, they were expert makeup artists and loved showing off their skills to a more appreciative audience than a church full of mourners. Past Halloweens, they'd painted his face goblin-green, vampire-white, and zombie-gray. Once, even into a masque of red death. Of course, he had to lie down on his back for them to work their magic.

"No. It's okay. I might get tired of it, and I can always take off a mask."

"Your call. Well, go ahead and put it on. I didn't dig your grandfather's old robe out of the attic for you to tuck it into bed. Your friends will be over any minute and it'll be curfew before you know it."

Douglas quickly wriggled into the black robe, grabbed the scythe, and snapped on the mask before walking into the bathroom to check himself in the mirror. As he pulled the hood over his head and stared into familiar eyes in the unfamiliar context of pale bone-colored plastic, he had an involuntary mental image of himself at the base of the ladder staring up at his window in infernal disappointment.

The back door croaked out its ugly buzz, and he ran down the hall past his parents who were sitting in the kitchen, to answer it.

"You sure you don't need a coat? It's like January out there," said Mrs. Mortimer.

"No, it'll ruin my costume. I'll be fine."

"The robe's pretty heavy," offered Mr. Mortimer.

"And you're sure we can't paint your face?" asked Douglas's mother.

"No, for the thousandth time."

"Okay. Have a good time. Stick with your friends. Be back by curfew. If you get any caramels, save them for me."

"Okay. Bye." Douglas grabbed the white pillowcase that his father was holding out to him and dashed down the back stairs. To avoid tripping, he lifted the hem of his robe a few inches in a way that Death, himself, would never have been caught dead doing.

On the back porch, a pair of child abominations stood waiting. One was a large raven: black pants, black shoes, black shirt, black felt feathers covering its arms and back, and a black half-mask with a long black beak obscuring the human face beneath. It didn't, however, hide the long black hair that hung loose down to the feathered shoulders. Strips of reflective safety tape adorned Audrey's pants like creases and matched a strip on both her chest and back. It only somewhat ruined the effect of the carrion bird costume.

Lowell wore two long brown horns on either side of his head—the same horns he had on when pranking Douglas's class—and a large, gold ring dangled from his nostrils. A plastic double-bladed ax with a short handle was propped on his shoulder. Minotaur. A skinny one, and one dressed casually in jeans and a sweater with holes in the elbows, but the man-bull monster of ancient Greek myth nevertheless. Like Douglas, each horrid creature carried a bag of some sort. Lowell's was a striped pillowcase. Audrey carried an obviously mom-made cloth Halloween sack, black with an orange jack-o'-lantern stitched onto it.

"Man, nice costume," said Lowell.

"Thanks. You guys look awesome, too. Where's your little brother?" Douglas asked Lowell. They usually found a way to ditch him every year, but he figured that they wouldn't be able to this year.

"Dad's on patrol, so he figured since he was walking the streets anyway, he'd keep Josh with him."

"Wise move," said Audrey. "By splitting you two up he's got a greater chance of at least one of you surviving the night."

Lowell flared his nostrils at her, making the large ring swing slightly. "Shall we go do some serious candy damage to our pancreases?"

The Raven, the Minotaur, and the Grim Reaper walked out of the mortuary and immediately started canvassing the neighborhood. The early darkness of the autumn season was freshly laid, and there was a full moon out, although it had to fight with a sky full of large clouds to get the best view of the festivities. Douglas tightened his hood a bit. His mother was right about the temperature.

Normally, Cowlmouth was relatively deserted after sunset, even in those past days when it didn't have a killer roaming its streets. However, on this All Hallow's Eve, monsters thronged the streets. Tiny witches, miniature ghosts, shrunken ghouls, and other creatures of absurd scale all flowed down the sidewalks, stopping at each door with entreaties and half-joking threats. But the air, instead of being heavy with groans and growls and shrieks, vibrated with the chatter of children as they, behind masks and hoods and face paint, drew courage from their anonymity, from continually facing strangers in doorways and monsters on streets, and from their brimming bags of candy.

And in the midst of all that costumed revelry, a ghastly gang of three were having more fun than they'd expected to, almost forgetting the dark pall that the Day Killer had left over the town. In fact, they had been filling their sacks for almost an hour and a half and not a one of them had mentioned the words *murder* or *killer* even once.

At one point, Douglas stumbled into an apparition staggering down the sidewalk. Douglas's first impression was of a headless man in a period costume carrying under his arm an evil-looking jack-o'-lantern. It took him a few seconds to register the badly cut eye-holes in the oversized fake shoulders that covered up the wearer's head.

"Boo," said the headless specter, which, under the circumstances, was a perfectly acceptable acknowledgement in lieu of "excuse me," before running off, presumably to chase after schoolteachers.

Down another street, the group found themselves embroiled in a candy corn fight between a pair of witches and a group of Pilgrims. After heaving a few snack-sized candy bar grenades into the fray, the three-some made it safely down the road.

In front of Town Hall, near the statue of the founder, burned the orange heart of Cowlmouth's Halloween, a monstrous jack-o'-lantern. The bulbous, warty creature sat heavily on a stack of wooden pallets. It had wide, angular features that glowed and glowered. Through them, a halogen lamp could be seen giving life to the jack-o', its demon-tail extension cord trailing behind its bulk through a hole bored into the shell. The electric pumpkin stared at the monsters that streamed past as if they were its personal minions. A thin line of yellow police tape formed a magic square around the pump-kin, keeping those minions at bay.

The trio stopped at the tape. A cardboard sign beside it labeled the winner of the Cowlmouth Fall Carnival as PIPKIN'S SOUL. Douglas stared at it for a few moments and then looked at the tip of his plastic scythe. "Anybody have a pocketknife?" Audrey reached a feathered hand into her costume to pull out the orange-handled blade with the emergency medical services insignia, the same tool she'd brandished at Cowlmouth Cemetery. Douglas took the knife, dropped his candy bag and scythe, and adjusted his skull mask to make sure it covered his face. With a quick look around, he slipped easily under the tape.

"Whoa, whoa, where you going?" Lowell called after him.

Douglas didn't answer. He just walked straight up to the demon gourd. He pulled open the knife and bent over the pumpkin. When he stood up, there was a letter cut into its orange flesh, right beside its evil grin—a D.

"Holy hockey sticks," was all he heard behind him.

Douglas took a step back, admired his handiwork, and then slowly walked back, tossing Audrey the knife and ducking under the tape. As his two friends stared at him, he said, "We're facing our monsters tonight, right?"

Eventually, the Raven and the Grim Reaper and the Minotaur found their sacks filled with enough candy to last them until the next Halloween. They jumped out of the seemingly unending stream of tiny terrors and into the deep entryway of a defunct furniture store that was one of the few havens from Halloween in all downtown. In that bubble of calm, they dropped their bags to the concrete with loud thumps. Audrey followed the bags with her own thump while Lowell and Douglas saluted each other with their plastic weapons and commenced sparring.

"Man, this feels like the best Halloween ever," Lowell said as he parried a pass from Douglas's scythe.

"Everybody seems really into it," agreed Douglas, aiming for one of Lowell's horns.

"What next?" asked Audrey. "Curfew?"

"No way, man. Ow!" Lowell dropped his ax, paying for it with a smart slap across his knuckles from Douglas's scythe. "This is probably my last Halloween."

Douglas dropped his scythe to his side and raised the skull mask so that it sat on his head. "What do you mean?"

"Getting too old for this. Might be too old already."

"Yeah, you're right. I don't think many other seventh graders went out this year." Audrey reached into her bag, fished out a piece of candy, and, without looking at it, unwrapped it and tossed it into her beak.

"There was no way I was going to skip trick-or-treating on a Halloween with a genuine murderer in town. Next year, I won't have that excuse. Probably."

In the gorgeous orange and black of the moment, as the flow of trick-or-treaters mobbed past about ten feet away, "a genuine murderer in town" was the least unsettling part of that statement to Douglas. He looked through the costumes at his friends. At Lowell, at Audrey, at Lowell again. *Lowell's last Halloween*, he thought. He couldn't imagine trick-or-treating without his best friend, which meant this was probably Douglas's last Halloween, too.

"We should watch some scary movies after curfew. My place," he offered.

"Now *that's* Halloween. Horror movies at a funeral home," said Audrey, picking at a bit of feather that dangled above her eye.

"Anybody got a jawbreaker? I kind of want a jawbreaker," said Lowell, dropping to the ground and digging around in his pillowcase. Audrey dove into her personal hoard to see what she could come up with. Douglas didn't move. His bag sat lonely on the stoop. He was staring out the entryway, trying to point a shaking finger at the street.

A tall, robed form had strode darkly across the entryway. It was just for a few seconds, but in those seconds, things seemed to go wavy—strange—as if Douglas's inner ears had shut down. He could barely hear what his friends were saying.

"That was him," Douglas finally mustered.

"What?" mumbled Audrey, chewing on the decapitated head of a cinnamon bear.

"Him. The Day Killer. He just walked right past us."

CHAPTER
21

All three ran to the edge of the entryway, peering around it like monsters in a closet waiting for a child-victim to enter its bedroom.

"Where is he?" Lowell hissed.

Douglas raised one hand and slowly pointed a finger as if he really were the Grim Reaper calling out the soon-to-be deceased. The dark figure, a larger version of Douglas, continued down the street. The costume blended well into the crowd of ghouls. "We're going after him, right?" Douglas was almost surprised to hear that the words were his own.

"I might be a little candy-drunk, but I totally think we should," said Audrey.

"I could be wrong." He didn't think he was.

Lowell cracked a grin large enough that it almost dislodged his nose ring. "Of course we're going after him. Wrong or not, we've got to find out. Come on." He reached out and snagged Audrey's arm as she jumped out onto the sidewalk. "Don't forget your bags. We're no longer trick-or-treating. But we are pretending to trick-or-treat."

At first, they all stuck close together, but at Lowell's instruction, the group spread out into a loose snake, making it easier to cut through the Halloween crowd. Each person kept their eyes on the friend ahead of him or her. Whoever was in front kept their eyes on the dark form. Lowell started out in the lead, but the group alternated so that if the hooded figure turned around, there was less chance he'd suspect he was being followed.

When it was Douglas's turn, he tried to pick out some identifying detail about the figure, or what it was that made him so sure, despite the brief glance, that it was the monster that had chased him that cemetery night. But there was nothing. Just a hump of black weaving through a tide of monsters. Nothing strange. At least on a Halloween night. No masks swiveled as the figure passed. Nobody took off running in terror.

But all Douglas could think was that the Day Killer was inches away from hundreds of potential victims.

If he was the Day Killer.

Maybe he was just somebody's dad trying to find his kids. Douglas tried his hardest to convince himself that was true.

A few blocks later, they found themselves on more residential streets in an area that bordered Druid Park, a forest that started at the edge of town and extended almost all the way to Main Street. The clumps of trick-or-treaters thinned here, so the Ghastlies stuck closer together. Every once in a while, they found it necessary to climb a porch and do some actual trick-or-treating to keep from looking out of place.

Eventually, the hooded figure turned down a side street, disappearing around the corner of a house.

Lowell stuck his arms out to stop the other two, counted off a reasonable amount of time, and then dropped them. The group raced to the corner, peering down the street.

"Hockey sticks!" whispered Lowell.

The long street sloped down into darkness and was completely empty of candy-laden monsters. The night's trick-or-treaters had already passed through this neighborhood like a pestilence, leaving each house barren and devoid of treats. All that they'd left in their wake were a few torn paper skeletons dangling from porch overhangs, some discarded apples in the gutter, and a few flimsy candy wrappers scratching across the street in the breeze.

A lone, dark figure walked down the sidewalk, getting farther and farther ahead and blinking in and out of existence under the glow of the street lights.

"There's no way we can follow him down there without him realizing it," said Lowell, pacing as he swung his ax. "We're going to lose him."

"We should call somebody. Your dad, maybe," said Audrey, pulling her phone from somewhere among her feathers.

"We could. But by the time he got here, that guy will be safe at home or eight streets away or hiding in the middle of Druid Park. And all he has to do is ditch the robes and he could hide even better than that. Worse, we don't have any proof that he is the Day Killer, nothing except Douglas's word. And I definitely don't want to explain to my dad why we all believe that. What's the killer doing out on a Monday, anyway? It doesn't make any sense."

"Maybe he ran out of toothpaste," said Douglas.

"Still, other than Doug, this is the closest anybody has ever been to the killer and lived," protested Audrey. "We have to remember where we are. We should start looking from here the next time we patrol." She craned her head to look up at the looming green sign attached to the telephone pole at the corner. "Chatman Street."

"Wait." Douglas flipped up his skull mask to check the name of the street, himself. *Why does that name seem so familiar? Something about . . .*

"Wait for what?" asked Audrey.

Douglas didn't answer. He just kept looking at the green aluminum rectangle. And then he had it. "We're not going to lose him. I think I know where he's going," he said quietly. "Death House."

"That's what I call your house," said Audrey. "I mean, before I knew you, of course. Now I call it Doug's Death House."

"You're stepping on an explanation," Lowell said to her.

"It's an abandoned house somewhere on this street. It's supposed to be haunted. Would make an ideal hide-out for somebody trying to hide between murders."

"How many Halloweens have we been through together, Doug?" Lowell spoke the question in a strange monotone, staring at his finger as he ran it over the blunt edge of his plastic ax.

"I don't know. Like three or four." Douglas looked at Audrey, who shrugged in a "He's your best friend" kind of way.

Lowell continued examining the details of his prop weapon. "And all this time you've been holding out on me? You've had a genuine haunted house in your back pocket, and you've never brought it up? Not even once? There are laws governing friendship, and I'm pretty sure that's a severe transgression of them. Did Moss and Feaster tell you about it?"

"My dad, actually. And it was only a few weeks ago. Things have been kind of crazy since then."

"Yeah, like following-a-serial-killer-down-a-deserted-street-on-Halloween-night crazy," said Audrey.

"Tell us about Death House," insisted Lowell.

Douglas fiddled with the hood of his robe, which had noosed itself around his neck too tightly for his comfort. "There's not much to say, honestly. Dad called it Death House. Said it was on Chatman Street near Druid Park. There were rumors of a family that was murdered there back when my great-grandfather ran the funeral home. He didn't tell me any ghost stories.

Just that when he was a kid, they used to pretend it was haunted because nobody lived there." He dropped his skull face back into place. "Somebody probably lives there now."

"Well," Lowell said, swinging his ax pensively, "I always thought Cowlmouth needed a haunted house. Let's go."

"What about curfew?" Douglas asked through the thin veneer of his plastic skull. "It can't be that far off."

"Man, if we catch the Day Killer, we'll never have a curfew ever again."

Douglas dropped his head and looked at a scrap of orange streamer that had torn loose from a set of decorations and been trampled into a dingy brown color. "He could have led us here, you know—to a deserted street. He could be hiding out there waiting for us."

"There are three of us," said Audrey. "You heard the Halloween rules. Three equals safety. Mathematics."

Douglas nodded. "Then let's go."

The three stood at the top of a hill, gazing down the steep incline that ended somewhere in the darkness below them.

"The street looks pretty long. Any idea where this Death House is exactly?" asked Lowell.

"I think Dad said it was at the bottom."

"Of course it is," said Lowell.

"We'll find it. Just look for the house with blood ooz-ing from its windows," Audrey remarked dryly.

"Okay, last chance for anybody to suggest the sensible thing. We could all go to Doug's and catch some fright flicks," said Lowell. Nobody replied. "Good. They can make fun of us for trick-or-treating past our expiration dates, but they sure as hockey sticks aren't going to make fun of us for chickening out on a haunted house. Or a serial killer." They were bold words, but Douglas couldn't help but notice that Lowell was suddenly carrying the toy ax like it was real. He tightened his own grip on his scythe.

As they walked, the three automatically leaned back a few degrees to adapt to the descent. The streetlamps were on, but a bit too widely spaced to do too much other than make the darkness around them deeper. Even Audrey's reflective safety tape seemed muted. They could just see that the street was bordered on either side by large, rambling houses shoved close together, each shaped with unnecessarily extravagant arches, tall pillars and broad porches. All were visibly run-down and had been rebuilt with mismatched building materials, the mark of houses that had lived through too many decades. They were set high enough above the road that the only access to the front doors was long flights of steps. Were some giant monster to sweep away those steps with a pass of its claw, the occupants would be as effectively trapped as a bald Rapunzel in a tower. Behind the houses on their right, they could make out the tall, dark trees of Druid Park, making it seem like they were farther from the civilization of downtown than they actually were.

As they walked quietly down the hill, empty lots took the place of houses, like missing teeth in a rotting smile. Eventually, the empty spaces outnumbered the houses, until the trio finally arrived at the bottom of the street. It dead-ended in a cul-de-sac more like the outer boundary of the world than the end of a street. A single, terrifying house stood at the far end. Death House.

CHAPTER 22

If any house wore its haunted on the outside, Death House did.

Every wall bowed inward, except the ones that bowed out. Every window and door was twisted, bordered by enormous gaps like a badly put-together jigsaw puzzle. Death House's three chimneys were stained black from either ages-old soot or the terrified demons that expelled themselves from whatever dark heart kept this place standing against all the laws of physics. The house crouched more than it stood, as if it were nursing the injuries of its broken timbers and chasm-cracked foundation. Its roof sagged deep enough in the middle to relocate its attic somewhere to the third floor. And it made sounds . . . empty whistles and creaks and insect noises and faint, unidentifiable wails that continued even when the breeze slackened. Around the house, the earth had gone back to a primeval state in which three-foot-high grasses and black trees with long gnarled roots hid countless generations of twisted evolution, like some evil Galapagos.

"Ho. Lee. Crow," whispered Audrey. "How come I've never seen this place before?"

"It must only exist on Halloween," Lowell whispered back.

"It must've been abandoned for a hundred years. Like the town just let it sit here to rot, hoping one day it would dust into nothing and disappear," said Douglas. "Something horrible definitely happened here."

Audrey pushed her beak onto the top of her head. "So, do we trick-or-treat it?"

"Only if you want poisoned candy," was Douglas's reply.

"Then what?"

"We at least have to look inside," replied Lowell. "See if this is the Day Killer's hideout. And, if it ends up just being a haunted house, then fine. We ended Halloween in style."

"Man, I don't think my legs would listen to me even if I really wanted to walk up to that place," said Douglas.

"Please, Cemetery Boy. It's not that hard," said Audrey. "Three of us, remember?"

"For now," said Douglas ominously. "Then there'll be two. Then one. And then . . . the end."

"You're being silly. Besides, if we're going to miss curfew, let's make it worth it."

"Here goes nothing," said Lowell, edging closer to the gates. "Wish I had my baseball bat."

"Wait. I'll go first," said Audrey. She made a show of settling her raven mask back into place and heaving her black and orange candy sack over her shoulder before approaching the tall, threatening gates. At least, they'd been gates at one time. Now they were little more than a chaos of rusted, bent, and broken shafts of black iron that encircled the house like a stunted species of wild thorn bush. They seemed more "No Trespassing" sign than an actual "No Trespassing" sign. Audrey slid easily through one of the gaps and turned around. "I said I'll go first, not I'll go by myself."

Douglas and Lowell looked at each other and then followed.

Inside, they had to step over the smashed corpses of pumpkins that somebody had tossed over the gate, but mostly they waded more than walked, the long weeds brushing the bottoms of their elbows and twigs snapping beneath their sneakers. Douglas looked down and could barely make out flagstones from what had once been a walkway. It was hard to imagine that once upon a time people wanted a path to the house. Above them, the crooked black limbs of trees stretched bitterly toward the moon overhead, which had already escaped behind a sky that had grown solid with clouds.

Finally, they arrived at rickety porch steps that jutted into the weeds like a boat dock on a stagnant lake. Without discussion, they took turns tiptoeing up the decaying stairs, each board sagging beneath their slight weight, threatening to swallow them into whatever dark nether region gaped beneath the house.

Once on the porch, they discovered that it wasn't much safer than the stairs had been. Where the floorboards weren't loose, they were rotten; where not rotten or loose, they were completely missing. The friends could almost see the thin, flaking columns trembling in their efforts to hold up the porch roof. A large door was flanked by two tall windows that were cracked in spiderweb patterns, and from which dangled the remnants of shutters.

Lowell grabbed the cuff of his right sleeve with his right hand and rubbed a clean spot at eye level onto one of the windows. He leaned in and, shielding his eyes with his hands, tried to see through the interior grime and mold and cracks into the house itself. Douglas lifted his mask and did the same on the opposite pane. It was like looking underwater in the dark. All he could see were vague shapes that could have been either furniture or otherworldly creatures. Every once in a while, he detected motion as old rags of curtains quivered in the gusts that tore through the many holes in the walls.

"What do you guys see?" asked Audrey impatiently.

"Spooky stuff," answered Douglas.

"Here, my turn—" She was cut off by a quiet exclamation from Lowell.

"There's somebody in there," he whispered. Douglas couldn't remember ever hearing Lowell sound so small.

"Shut up," said Audrey.

Douglas instantly stuck his face back to the glass and caught the brief impression of a man-shaped shadow moving in an unmistakable man-type fashion.

"I'm serious. I saw a person move in there. Did you see it, Doug?" Douglas nodded and allowed Audrey to push him out of the way so she could look inside. "I don't see anything."

"It was only for a few seconds," Lowell replied.

"That means he's in there," mumbled Audrey.

"He's in there," returned Lowell, in a much different tone of voice. "Come on, we have to get to another window."

"What? What do you mean? We have to get out of here," Douglas said urgently.

"No way. We need to see who the Day Killer is. This is what we've been waiting for. Who knows how much longer he'll be here. All we need is to see his face, and then we'll have something to tell the coffee-drinkers."

Lowell dropped his bag of candy and cleared the porch steps in a single jump, landing in a splash of weeds. After a brief glance at Audrey, who returned his uncertain look, Douglas followed with much less exuberance, leaving his own hard-wrought plunder forgotten in a heap on the porch.

They ran to the side window, jockeying for position in front of the glass.

Douglas couldn't see anything.

"The back," said Lowell. It seemed even darker at the rear of the house, with the weeds almost twice as tall as the ones on the front lawn, but they were able to get up close to the back wall, where they discovered that the first-story windows there were all boarded up.

"Upstairs." Lowell pointed at a second-floor window, right above a flat overhang that ran partway along the house. He threw his plastic ax into the weeds and said, "Doug, boost me."

Douglas stuck his scythe under his arm and crouched with cupped hands. Lowell stepped into them and then onto Douglas's shoulders, hugging the decaying wall shingles of the house before reaching his long, scrawny arms up to the edge of the overhang. Douglas heard him mutter something about termites as he heaved himself up. The overhang shook and sagged under his weight, but held.

"Do you see anything?" hissed Douglas.

"Not yet. Hold on." In the dim moonlight, he could barely make out Lowell among the shadows. He seemed to be crouching as close to the window as he could. "It looks like an old storage heap inside," Lowell whispered. "Hold on . . . I'm going to chance it." Douglas could see him fumbling around until a tiny cone of light cut through the gloom.

On top of the overhang, Lowell aimed the pocket flashlight at the window. Most of the dim light bounced back off the solid grime coating the glass. "There's not much. Some broken furniture, piles of trash, an old rocking horse that might be the scariest thing I've ever seen in my life. That's about it."

"All right, man. You checked. Now come on down," whispered Douglas.

"Okay. Just seeing if there's a better place to look inside." Douglas saw the flashlight beam traveling along the exterior wall of the house before flicking abruptly off. "Okay. I'm coming down. Look out below."

Lowell jumped.

Death House screamed.

CHAPTER

23

Lowell crashed down onto Douglas in a shower of crumbling shingles, the two boys disappearing with a collective grunt into the deep weeds. Douglas surfaced first, his face blanched white enough to glow in the darkness. "What was that noise?" he asked nobody and everybody, Lowell, the weeds, Death House, Halloween night. "Audrey! Where is she?"

Douglas took off for the front of the house, plowing through the weeds and around the corner to the front porch. It was empty except for three bags of candy. One of the bags, black with an orange jack-o'-lantern on it, had fallen on its side, a colorful jumble of sweets spilling across the porch and down through one of the missing floorboards. The front door was open, vibrating crookedly on its bottom hinge. Across the front yard, he saw a tall, black figure lumber heavily through an empty lot toward the woods of Druid Park. It carried something that seemed to be struggling against it. Something shiny and familiar flashed briefly in the light of a nearby street lamp.

"Call your dad!" yelled Douglas in Lowell's general direction while simultaneously breaking into a panicked run after the retreating shape. He had barely made it to the tree line, though, when he saw a tall form, lanky, horned, and breathing heavily, streak by on long legs to jump ahead into the forest.

Douglas quickly lost sight of the black figure, but he kept Lowell in his view the best he could while trying to avoid tripping over rocks or running into trees. It seemed like a race without an end, the black forest stretching on and on, and Lowell shrinking smaller and smaller in front of him. Soon enough, Douglas's lungs began dissolving, his calves started splitting, and the cold Halloween air began freezing his throat. Eventually, he lost Lowell, and his short legs finally stumbled to a halt.

Douglas leaned over and placed his hands on his

knees. His organs seemed to tumble into his throat, and he collapsed at the base of a tree, full of bitter failure and hoping desperately that Lowell would be able to catch up to the murderer before it was too late. While Douglas gasped for breath and fought back tears, he reached into his robe and pulled out a pocket flashlight identical to the one that Lowell had been using. It had been part of a set they had bought and divvied up for late night misadventures past. Shining the small beam around, he noted the usual dry leaves, fallen branches, moss, rocks, roots, little nocturnal beetles that twinkled as his flashlight beam reflected off their shiny shells . . . and something else.

Something startling.

A pair of hollow eyes stared at him from a pile of dead leaves.

It was a black mask, lined with feathers, with a long black beak . . . and it was about twenty-five feet away from the direction that Lowell had been running.

Douglas got up, brushed the leaves off his grandfather's robe, and rushed over to the mask. He picked it up by the beak, the broken elastic strap dangling from it like a tapeworm. He shined his flashlight on it and thought furiously. It couldn't be up to Lowell now. He was too far into the forest, running fast in the wrong direction.

It was up to him now. He started to feel nauseated and his eyes were getting wet, but he rubbed at his face and darted in the direction the beak mask seemed to point.

The thin beam of his flashlight did little against the darkness of the forest. The full moon had already given up its attempt at a vigil, barely glimmering through the cloud cover. Douglas hurried as fast as he could, scraping his hands on rough bark, feeling his skin pierced here and there by the webs of brambles. He kept going, exhausted, uncertain of what to do. Uncertain of what he *could* do except keep going.

Eventually, he noticed a blue, flickering glow ahead. His mind immediately turned to the stories of wood imps that Moss and Feaster had shared. The kind that go for your eyeballs and keep eating until they leave through the soles of your feet. He turned off his flashlight and crept as softly as he could. As he neared the source of the blue glow, he heard muffled noises. Hiding behind a tree, he was glad he'd talked his parents out of making him put reflective tape on his dark cloak.

From behind the tree, Douglas could see the source of the light clearly. It was an electric bug killer, its caged bulb flickering and zapping a brave and solitary battle against the uncountable insect hordes of the woods. Looking further, he saw that it was hanging from a tree at the far end of a backyard. He was at the edge of the forest.

The house at the front of the yard was dark. They weren't welcoming any more trick-or-treaters. At the back edge of the property was a picnic area with a table and chairs and a fire pit. Looking up, Douglas only saw the dark underside of a vast bank of cloud. Without the full moon for competition, the bug killer threw an unreal aura of blue light about twenty feet into the forest, deep enough for Douglas to make out a large, dark shape crouching in the undergrowth.

At first, Douglas couldn't quite see what the shape was doing, but he could hear it whispering, the same sound that he had heard when he was being chased. The sound made Douglas want to run back to his house, to Lowell's house, even to Death House. But Audrey . . . Audrey!

He looked closer and could see something bright winking underneath the dark shape . . . the reflective tape on Audrey's raven costume—the same tape he had glimpsed in the lamp light as the figure left the haunted house in its wake. It was flashing in the blue electric nimbus as she struggled.

As Douglas's eyes finally adjusted, he saw what the black shape was doing. In its black-gloved hand, it held a wicked knife, point up like it was a candle at a vigil. Its hooded head was bent down close to Audrey's face. The monster was whispering to her.

The knife blade lowered. Audrey screamed.

In that exact moment, Douglas stopped observing, stopped being uncertain. His lungs reappeared and his calves sewed themselves solid and the furnace of his boyhood anger melted the frozen interior of his throat. He raised high into the night the plastic scythe that he still held and, running as fast as he could, threw his entire measly eighty pounds at the monster with a feral yell.

Had the Day Killer been alert—had he not been so distracted by the child-raven beneath him—he might have parried the small, black-robed missile with little effort. As it was, Douglas was an entire gutter of bowling balls hurtling at the speed of a playground sprint toward his dark target. The impact pulled a heavy grunt from the Day Killer's chest, knocking him a dozen feet away. The knife flew into the air, gleaming briefly in the bug killer light, before its flicker was extinguished in the thick carpet of leaves on the forest floor.

The impact had knocked Douglas to the ground in the opposite direction, the scythe sliding from his hand and scraping across the leaves. The thin plastic skull mask that had been perched on top of his head the entire chase slipped down crooked over his face, obscuring half of it and blinding one eye as surely as if he'd poked it out on a branch. But he didn't need to see clearly at that point. He only needed his voice.

"Run, Audrey!"

She didn't.

She jumped up, but her feet remained planted in the dark leaf litter. Her hand was on her cheek. She removed it and stared at her palm. On her cheek was a blotch of red that was black in the blue light shining on her face.

The Day Killer didn't move, either. He sat there, panting heavily from deep within the black hood he wore, so like Douglas's own costume. Even though Douglas couldn't see his face, it seemed as if the Day Killer was looking at him, staring. That was all. Staring. And then three words trickled like sewer water out of the dark hole of the hood.

"Sick of sun."

One single moment too late, Douglas jumped up to go to Audrey. The Day Killer moved with predator speed and grabbed him by the face, the skull mask coming off easily in his gloved hand and snapping in two as he closed his fist. His other hand grabbed Douglas's arm, almost snapping it, as well. The Day Killer threw the fractured skull to the ground and began scrabbling through the leaves with his free hand, searching for the lost knife.

Douglas tried to pull away from the black mass of the serial killer, but couldn't free himself. Instead, the killer pulled Douglas closer.

Then he lunged forward.

Douglas screamed.

The killer continued past him, falling to the ground. On his back, Audrey had one arm around his neck and the other slamming a fist into his hooded head as she pushed him to the ground with her entire body. She screamed, "Douglas, a D!" It was a strange battle cry, but her attack was effective. She'd caught the killer off-balance, one hand on Douglas and one stretched deep into the leaf cover. As he dropped face first to the ground with a muffled exclamation, his hand released Douglas.

Audrey jumped back and whispered, "Run."

And they did.

Douglas ran despite every branch slapping him in the face and every root twisting at his ankle. Ran despite the fact that he could barely see a single stride in front of him. Ran despite the fact that his robe kept twisting around his legs, threatening to send him sprawling. Ran because it mattered. Ran . . . by himself.

He thought that he'd heard Audrey following, but a quick glance over his shoulder showed the black form of the killer growing bigger behind him, ready to swallow him up. Ready to cut a letter into his face.

Douglas ran faster.

But he could only run so far before his short legs would be overtaken by longer ones, or before his body collapsed in exhaustion.

He realized he had been running parallel to the edge of the forest, and could see houses and lawns lit by streetlamps and the general glow of the town reflected off the underside of the clouds. He made a sudden exit from the woods, cut fast through a backyard and around a house. Spying a row of close-set rhododendron bushes covered in fake spiderwebs lining the front of the house, he dived behind them and settled into a dark corner beside the porch.

As he crouched behind the bushes, each second a fraying cord tied to a guillotine blade, he waited for the strange panting, for grasping hands to plunge into the bushes, for a knife blade already red from the blood of his friend to slide easily through the leaves.

Finally, silence piled on silence until it was so heavy that he had to move to get out from under it. He inched himself around one of the bushes and parted a few branches with his fingers. The street was empty. The houses were dark. He looked toward the adjacent doorway, gauging the height of the raised porch and high railing that barred the shortest distance between him and it. Like the rest of the houses, it was also dark. But it was his nearest possible sanctuary.

Douglas slowly stood up. He summoned the courage to slip around the bushes and leap the front steps to the door when, down the road, in the ghostly light of a street lamp, he saw a silhouette that scared his breath down into his throat and buckled his knees, folding him silently back down into the dirt.

It was only a few seconds of terror because, like an afterimage floating behind the back of his eyelids, Douglas could see that the silhouette was off. Too thin. Too familiar. Too pointy.

It had horns.

A different kind of fear enveloped Douglas. Any second, the Day Killer would come streaking into the neighborhood, and there was Lowell, on the street, out in the open, completely unaware of how close the monster was.

So Douglas leapt from the bushes and took off after him.

Lowell, apparently startled by the dark-robed shape erupting out of the shadows, bolted down the street.

Douglas felt hard pavement slam under his sneakers as he chased after his friend. He wasn't trying to catch up to him, not really. Just trying to get him out of the area. He didn't want to yell after him for fear that the killer would find them both. He just kept running.

Before the strange race had gone two blocks, Lowell stopped suddenly and turned around.

"You're kind of small for a serial killer," panted Lowell. "Why didn't you say something?" He bent over to catch his breath, grabbing the horns off his head and the large dangling nose ring out of his nostrils before dropping them to the street, where they landed with soft clacks of plastic. He had lost the ax at some point, and the hole in the right elbow of his sweater had pulled into a long tear. A shallow red scratch ran down the length of his exposed forearm. "I lost the killer and Audrey. I called Dad, but I couldn't just wait around. I've been trying to find . . . anybody."

Douglas eyed the open street around them. "I found her. She got away. I think she's okay, but she ran off in a different direction than me. Right now, though, we've got to keep going. He's here. The Day Killer. Somewhere nearby. He chased me out of the forest."

"All right. Your house is probably closer." Lowell pointed down the road in the opposite direction.

A direction from which a large hooded figure was barreling toward them.

CHAPTER 24

The boys flew. Terror feathered their arms and the black street beneath their sneakers liquefied into a blurring torrent of tar. Lowell, with his longer legs, took the lead, but without even speaking to each other, they both knew where they were headed.

Soon, the large, familiar black gates loomed in front of them. The murderer had made almost the entire town of Cowlmouth seem alien to Douglas and Lowell, but the cemetery—Cowlmouth Cemetery—was their park, their backyard, their playground, their haven. Douglas and Lowell knew the stones of that final resting place as intimately as if every one of them marked the grave of a family member.

They veered away from the locked front gates toward the low side wall of the cemetery. Tonight, the entire wall of Cowlmouth Cemetery was alive with faces. Arranged across the top of the stone divider was a line of leering, grinning, scowling, grimacing jack-o'-lanterns. It was a town tradition. Inside, many of the graves would be sprouting miniature pumpkins instead of the usual memoriam of flowers. Halloween was a great night to remember the dead.

Also a great night to avoid becoming one of them.

Atop the outer wall, the innards of the jack-o'-lanterns flickered with hot souls. Later that night, Moss and Feaster would douse them, as surely as they buried bodies at any other time. The boys vaulted over the wall, decapitating it of a few of its jack-o'-lanterns, which hit the soft turf on the other side and rolled to a halt at the foot of some of the gravestones, prematurely snuffed.

As soon as Douglas's feet hit the well-fed grass, he found his second wind, as if he were being energized by the cemetery he knew so well.

They continued running, Lowell half a grave plot ahead, both boys deftly avoiding the tombstones and statuary. Douglas heard a heavy thud near the bare spot in the jack-o'-lantern line atop the wall. He didn't look back. Despite his renewed vigor, he felt as if he weren't running fast enough, as if the dead were reaching from their graves and grabbing at his ankles, slowing him down. Any second, the Day Killer would pounce on him.

"Hide," Douglas whisper-shouted at Lowell's back as he dived behind a tall, thick obelisk. He saw Lowell pull a controlled fall on the far side of a large sarcophagus topped by a pair of stone children, one at each end like they were riding a seesaw.

Douglas leaned back against the obelisk, trying to silently catch both his breath and his courage. He tilted his head back and saw that the large, pointed column was topped by a delicate stone angel eternally blowing a long trumpet. It was meant to represent the Last Trump, the divine blast at which the dead were supposed to rise at the end of the world.

Right now, Douglas could use the help of a cemetery full of the resurrected dead.

As he continued to stare up at the statue and the clouded sky above it, he felt small bits of cold hitting his face. Looking down at his costume, he saw a galaxy of tiny white stars blinking into existence on the black cloak. Snow. In October. On Halloween.

He risked a peek around the obelisk.

Against the light from the lampposts outside the cemetery gates, he saw the tall silhouette of their pursuer, the lightly falling snow a meager buffer between them. Seeing him standing there like a piece of funerary art, there was no doubt that this was, as Moss had said, a different type of monster. A human one.

Suddenly, the murderer's arm arced quickly upward and then sharply downward into a small pumpkin perched atop a tombstone. Whatever was in his hand stuck deep into the pumpkin's flesh. As he brought back his hand the skewered pumpkin came with it. He pounded the pumpkin hard against the tombstone with a dead-sounding thud, and another, and another, until the pumpkin fell away in two rough halves. The Day Killer had found his knife.

Douglas knew he and Lowell couldn't stay where they were. They needed to find a better hiding place. He also knew exactly where that was. They just had to get to it.

Slinking back away from the obelisk, Douglas crawled toward Lowell, who was sitting with his back to the stone coffin holding his head in his hands. As Douglas got close enough to whisper in his ear, Lowell jumped.

"It's snowing," Lowell whispered in surprise.

Only a couple inches of space separated their faces. Lowell looked pale and lost and his eyes seemed slightly swollen. "Grassley," was all Douglas said to him. Lowell nodded slowly.

The boys tried to keep as many monuments between themselves and the killer as they could. Moving slowly from tombstone to tombstone like grave ghouls, they finally found themselves in front of a row of mausoleums cut into the side of a hill. The large stone houses for the dead were all about the same size, although they varied wildly in design, from simple, blank facades to church-like structures dominated by stained glass windows. Toward the end of the row was a relatively unnoticeable-looking mausoleum with a copper door green from age. It was embossed with grapevines that dangled down its surface like the tentacles of an octopus. The name Grassley was inscribed above the door. Like the rest of the mausoleums, this one was supposed to be locked, but as long as Douglas could remember, it never had been. He opened the door.

A scream like that of a murder victim ripped across the night, echoing off the tombstones and statues and mausoleums. Douglas felt his blood turn to powder and his own cold fear merge with the cold of the dead and the cold of the night. An automatic look at Lowell revealed his friend's similar reaction. He hadn't realized how loud those ancient hinges were when he and Lowell had hung out there in the daytime on their many adventures. Douglas ducked inside, followed close by Lowell. Each wincing, the boys tugged the door closed behind them with a second screeching murder.

Inside were two concrete sarcophagi, a his and a hers, each labeled with names and dates from the 18th century, William Grassley on one side and his wife Morgana on the other. In the walls were interred other members of the Grassley family. Douglas knew that from memory, though. All he could see right now was solid darkness. He felt his way for the bench he knew to be built into the back wall and sat down heavily on it, brushing some of the snow off his cloak and pulling out his flashlight. As he dragged its beam around the tiny interior, he felt Lowell drop down beside him.

The pale light slid across the walls and the two sarcophagi and the inside of the brass door, which was unadorned except for a few intersecting lines of studs. All the boys had for company was a family centuries dead and their own terrified thoughts. For Douglas, as seemed to be the way for the past month and a half, all of those thoughts were questions: How did this happen? Was Audrey safe? What did *sick of sun* mean? He chose an easy one to start with.

"Did you bring your flashlight?"

"I lost it when I jumped off Death House." Lowell's voice sounded odd.

"Are you okay?" Without thinking Douglas aimed the light at Lowell's face. Lowell squinted and tried to wave the beam away. Douglas moved the light elsewhere with a mumbled apology.

"Am I okay? Are you okay? We're being chased by a killer . . . We'll probably die tonight."

Douglas didn't respond. He watched the pale circle of his flashlight beam as it haunted the inside of the mausoleum.

"I don't get it," Lowell said in a low voice, standing up and leaning against William Grassley's sarcophagus. "It's a Monday. He shouldn't have been out tonight. We never should have even seen him. Never tracked him back to Death House. The whole town thought he wouldn't be out tonight. Halloween was ours." That last sentence came out almost as a whimper.

"I shouldn't have said anything when I saw him," answered Douglas.

"Nope. You weren't wrong for that. You haven't been wrong since this whole thing started. I've been the one who's been wrong. I mean, I've been acting like the murders were the best thing to happen in this town since I moved here. I was excited by them. Felt like I was in a movie. Sure doesn't feel like a movie anymore." Lowell was silent for a moment. "Man, I really should have listened to you. We should have gone right to my dad after the killer chased you to your house. I'm such an idiot."

"Hey, I didn't even listen to me. We made the same bad calls together."

"Bad calls," Lowell hissed. "He could have killed Audrey tonight. You're sure she got away?"

Douglas shined the light on his own face so that Lowell could see him nod. He didn't offer any details.

"I'm sorry, man. I can't believe I was having so much fun."

They let the conversation die out. After a while, Lowell asked, "What are we going to do?"

"Wait, I guess. Wait him out. Wait until morning. Wait until the police find us. Or Moss and Feaster." Douglas knocked the heel of the flashlight on Morgana Grassley's sarcophagus. "The patience of the dead."

Douglas continued to let the flashlight beam roam free. In its wanderings, it highlighted the curved ceiling, the inner handle of the door—a feature that had always amused him, giving him images of the dead going outside for a breath of fresh air. The light played along the rounded corners of the sarcophagi, the names on the lids. *Grassley* was engraved into each surface in large, ornate letters. Beneath each was a simple epitaph. *Loving Father, Loving Mother.* On the walls were the tombs of loving sons and daughters, beloved wives and husbands. As the light moved across the epitaphs and names, Douglas felt as if he were deciphering a coded message. He moved the light backwards across the epitaphs and they became foreign words. The circle of light wavered on a prominent *D* that led the word *Daughter.*

And Douglas remembered.

He remembered a dark shape lit in an eerie flickering blue light. He remembered the flash of a nasty knife. He remembered an eerie whispering like the monster was talking to his victim. And he remembered Audrey's odd battle cry, a statement that had made no sense. *Douglas, a D!* It was a letter he himself had carved into a pumpkin rind earlier that night.

Except now it did make sense.

No day of the week started with *D*.

Douglas understood. He had the key to the whole ghastly thing. A piece of information that had come straight from the monster, itself, leaking twice from the black hood of Cowlmouth's own private Grim Reaper.

"We're wrong about the murders."

Lowell squinted through the flashlight beam, trying to make out the dark boy behind it. "What do you mean?"

"The Day Killer. He's not the Day Killer. I mean, he is, but that shouldn't be his name."

"What are you talking about?"

"His pattern. The letters. We were wrong. Everybody was. Listen. When I found Audrey, the killer was taunting her."

"What was he saying?"

"I don't know. I couldn't make it out, but when she attacked him . . ."

"She attacked him?"

"Yeah, she attacked him to save me. But while she was doing that, she yelled something that didn't make any sense."

"There's a lot of that in this story."

"She said, 'Douglas, a *D*.' I think the killer told her what letter he was going to cut into her cheek."

"Oh no. Did he cut her?"

"No. I mean, I think he might have nicked her when I threw myself at him."

"You threw yourself at him?"

"Low . . . a *D*."

Lowell looked like he was listing something in his head. "No day starts with *D*."

"I know. But you know what does?"

Lowell looked at him, not even squinting in the flashlight beam that Douglas had dragged across him and then threw at the wall, highlighting a single word.

"Daughter."

Lowell didn't respond. Just waited.

"The killer isn't counting a week. He's creating a family. Mrs. Laurent's *M* wasn't for murder or monster or Monday . . . It was for mother. Mr. Rivet's *F* was for father. Marvin was the son. Audrey would have been the daughter. And me . . ."

"Another son." Something lit in Lowell's eyes that was almost visible in the sepulchral darkness. "That *S* on the giant pumpkin must've been meant for you. The killer was following you at the carnival. Not sick of sun. Not even s-u-n sun. You'd have been the *second son*."

Might still be, Douglas thought. "Why me?" was what he said instead.

"Man, the first time you saw him was at your house, which just happens to be where all of his victims ended up. That's got to be it. That's why he noticed you. You were just there, sharing a roof with his victims. Heck, he was probably at Mr. Stauffer's funeral, too. Everybody was."

"I must've handed him a program."

A disturbing sound penetrated the thick walls of the mausoleum, as if agreeing with the statement. It sounded like metal shaking against stone. As the boys listened, the sound repeated itself and got closer. Someone was trying the doors of the mausoleums. Not someone—the Day Killer. No, not the Day Killer. Not anymore. Some other name. Not that it mattered.

Panicked, Douglas flashed the beam around the inside of the mausoleum like it was a lightning bolt, looking for anything that could help them. The room was too small to offer a hiding place. Too stingy to offer a weapon.

"The sarcophagi," whispered Lowell frantically.

The boys tried to pry open the heavy stone lids on first William Grassley's and then Morgana's final resting places, but it would take a funeral's worth of pallbearers armed with crowbars to move either of those ancient stones.

Another rattle and scrape, closer.

They slumped on the altar.

"He's got us," Lowell said simply.

Douglas turned off the flashlight.

The two boys sat and listened to the sounds of door handles being rattled, of chains being tugged, of padlocks being shaken, each sound growing closer and closer as the killer moved down the row of mausoleums toward the one in which they hid. Douglas put an arm around Lowell's shoulders and could feel him shivering.

Another rattle and scrape, closer.

And the two boys sat.

Like cemetery statues.

Like grief-paralyzed mourners.

Like terrified children.

Like those who have given up all hope.

Finally, the bronze door in front of them shifted slightly in its concrete jamb with a loud scrape, and a vertical slit of night appeared. Lowell and Douglas looked at each other, and then Lowell gave Douglas a crooked grin.

Just as the hinges started to scream, the two boys bolted, throwing the entire weight of their bodies, their souls, and every heavy thought that had been burdening their brains that night straight at the door.

It flew open fast at the unexpected force, the scream of its hinges sharper and shorter as the heavy metal slab rebounded against whoever was on the other side. The boys exploded out into the cemetery, Douglas's hood and robe trailing behind him like a shadow clinging on for dear existence and Lowell like a charging bull sans horns or a scarecrow freshly unpegged.

And they ran.

Like mourners late for a funeral, they ran.

Like bodies newly risen from the dead.

Like terrified children.

Like the embodiments of hope.

And they ran in completely different directions.

At first, Douglas didn't realize they had separated. And he didn't know where he was running or if there was even a finish line to this race. But, as he saw the snow-dusted pumpkins on the graves, he remembered the jack-o'-lanterns on the wall. Someone would have to douse the flames: Moss and Feaster. He had to find Moss and Feaster.

Curfews didn't apply to monsters, and they didn't apply to those who fought monsters, either.

He risked a look back for Lowell, but didn't see him. He risked another for the killer, and didn't see him, either. The flakes were coming down heavier, and the entire cemetery glowed. While he'd been in the mausoleum, the ground had been coated in a thin film, not enough to sheath the dark points of the blades of grave grass, but enough that it was hard not to slip as he angled and re-angled through the labyrinth of monuments.

It was enough snow to reveal footprints, too, but Douglas figured there was nothing he could do about that. He put his head down and ran, sensing more than seeing the tombstones and statues that he nimbly steered around, concentrating on keeping his feet under him and his target ahead. Eventually, through the falling flakes, he could make out the most beautiful site in the world—an ugly, squat, triangular toolshed that was almost as old as the cemetery and twice as decayed as many of its residents. Built half-heartedly against a side wall, here was where Moss and Feaster kept all of their equipment. Here was where they were surely sheltering from the Halloween snow.

Douglas ran full speed into the warped wooden door, gray with age, and the ancient, brittle windows rattled at the impact. The door didn't give. Locked. After quickly wiping away the film of snow from a pane with the sleeve of his costume, he peered inside. Empty. Not even a coat on a peg. The snow seemed suddenly to penetrate his skin and congeal around his heart.

Wait. Too empty. Douglas didn't need another look inside to know what was missing. Where was Daisy? The large yellow backhoe loader should have been parked in the middle of the shed. Douglas looked around to see if it was nearby, but the snow was coming down harder now, thickening the air.

Thickening it enough that it hid the black form until it was almost on top of him.

"Second son," it hissed with an upraised hand that held death as surely as if it were the Grim Reaper's scythe.

Douglas ran. The monster ran. The sky snowed. The dead slumbered.

If felt to Douglas as if his lungs were stuffed with pine needles and the bones in his legs had crumbled and his skull was sloshing to the crown with boiling blood. He wanted to pick a grave and lie down. Instead, he squinted, looking, aching for something particular.

Finally, he saw it.

On a hillock in the distance, he could make out the silhouette of a dinosaur-like head stretching into the sky against the glow of the town. He ran for it, the monster panting steps behind him. Every sudden turn was that much more distance between him and the serial killer. Between him and death.

And it was that much closer to safety. Where Daisy was, that's where Moss and Feaster would be. He kept her raised backhoe in his sights.

Douglas charged through the cemetery's covered bridge, slowing down to soften the sound of his shoes against the wooden planks. He risked a look behind him. He didn't see the monster. Maybe the bridge was protection against more than headless horsemen. Exiting the other side and passing the dark chapel, he sped up again, running by another line of mausoleums and up the hill to the cemetery machine ... almost skidding on the snow into an open grave.

He should have known better. Wherever Daisy was, there was usually an open grave nearby. He looked around, but saw no sign of Moss or Feaster anywhere. On top of that, Daisy was dark, all her lights off.

He ducked around the many appendages of the vehicle and squatted down to hide on her far side, not knowing what to do next or where to go. He wondered where Lowell was. Wished he were here with him. No, wished Lowell was safe elsewhere. He should have run back to Death House instead of to the cemetery. That's where the police would be after Lowell had called them. He should have banged on every door in the surrounding neighborhood. Or shouted in the streets until everyone realized it wasn't a Halloween prank and came outside. He never should have told his friends he saw the monster in the first place. But now, alone except for thousands of corpses, he was going to be murdered. Douglas, the boy who got death, was facing it.

Yet there, crouched in the snow, his only shelter the cold yellow metal of a grave-digging machine, his only company a cemetery full of the dead and a pursuer that wanted him to end up the same way, Douglas did finally think he understood death. Natural death, unnatural death, murder, heart attack, car accident, dead in your sleep, dead in the ground. None of that was important. Death, whatever its form, whenever it happened, wasn't the point. Death was never the point.

In that strange calm that only cemeteries have, Douglas realized how much he wanted to live. He wanted to walk right down Main Street to get a hot caramel sundae at Sweeney's. Wanted to watch a movie at the theater with a big, warm tub of popcorn on his lap. Wanted to go to another Fall Carnival. To graduate to the next grade in school. He wanted to play video games. To listen to Moss's and Feaster's monster stories and Reverend Ahlgrim's eulogies. He wanted to be called Mortimer the Cadaver Kid. Wanted his mom to tousle his hair and to go on more removals with his dad. He wanted another of Dr. Coffman's lemon candies. And to see his great-grandfather's collection of funeral art in the sitting room. He wanted to polish the coffins in the showroom. To watch Eddie make a dead body beautiful. He wanted to get to know Audrey better. And he wanted to do all of that with Lowell, his best friend in the whole world, at his side.

But if he died tonight in the cold Halloween snow, at least he had known all those people and done all those things.

And that didn't feel like salvage. It felt like . . . somebody else's funeral.

There was a reason people went through the funeral ritual, why they followed the customs and picked out a casket or an urn, and held a service, and dug a hole or lit a fire. There was a reason why people grieved and cried and got together with loved ones. It wasn't play-acting or pretending.

It was living.

It was everything a dead person couldn't do. People are the most alive at funerals. "Not for the deceased." That's what his dad always said about the funeral business. It wasn't really about the dead or how they died or why they died. It was about continuing to live until your own death, however that happened.

Living was worth dying for. Even dying badly.

And that was exactly what he had to do.

Sitting there in the snow, cold metal against his back, the most horrible thought entered Douglas's head: *What if the killer can't find me?*

He'd been sitting there too long. He must have lost the monster in his race across the cemetery. That meant he might be safe. But if he were, the monster would find a different victim. And there was only one other victim in that cemetery.

Douglas had to make sure Lowell was safe.

He jumped up from the snow and clambered up the various protrusions on Daisy's flank until he found himself standing on the slippery metal of her roof. All around him, the cemetery was dark, although the dim light from the town gave vague forms to the headstones through the static of snow. The audience of graves waited expectantly. Douglas screamed the first thing that popped into his head.

"Second son!"

The two words sounded tiny, blown away by the wind, absorbed by the graves. He tried again, putting as much force into them as his freezing lungs could throw.

"Second son!"

Douglas strained his ears in the silence. He imagined he could hear the tiny flakes striking the stones. But no shadows moved. No snow parted. Not even an echo returned his cry. He would need a bonfire and a bullhorn to get anybody's attention.

Fortunately, he had Daisy. She gave off a lot of light. And made a lot of noise.

He scrambled from her roof and dived into her cab and the driver's seat. A plastic, severed hand dangled from the mirror. The windows were plastered with monster stickers. And surrounding him were enough knobs and buttons and levers to confuse an astronaut. He'd seen Moss and Feaster work Daisy a thousand times, and knew it was more an art than a science. But he did know how to turn the rickety, yellow beast on. He gave the keys dangling from the dashboard a twist. And, for the first time in the history of Daisy, she started on the first try, resurrecting into a glory of headlights and engine noise.

"Yes!" he shouted, high-fiving the severed hand.

A black hood popped up at the window. "Second son," it said as a streak of knife blade invaded the cab, tickling the fabric against Douglas's chest.

Douglas threw himself back against the cracked vinyl of the driver's seat. He looked down at his chest, expecting the worst, but saw only a tear in his thick robe. He looked at the hooded figure standing just outside Daisy's cab. The monster had pulled his hand back from the half-open window. His black robe was specked with snow as if he were wrapped in an indifferent universe.

"Second son," the voice repeated, colder than the graves, colder than the snow.

The monster lunged at him again, and Douglas squeezed himself back into the opposite corner, out of reach of the deadly blade. After a few failed swipes, the monster scrabbled at the handle. The door opened, and the monster lunged inward, just as Douglas kicked out his feet to parry the attack. His left foot struck the monster in the side of the head, for the second time that night pulling a grunt from the depths of the dark hood, and repelling the figure out of the cab. Douglas didn't even notice that he'd connected, continuing to kick his feet in terror. His right foot hit one of the levers and Daisy responded, swinging around on her axis. Her backhoe hit the monster, throwing him backward.

And then the monster disappeared.

A horrible thud, stark and final like the first spadeful of dirt on the polished lid of a coffin, soon followed.

Douglas froze for a long time as the snow seeped in through the open door, covering his robe in a layer of white that snuck into the openings to chill his skin. Finally, he jumped down from Daisy's cab.

He turned on his flashlight and saw the short trail first, like someone had brushed the snow from a four-foot section of dark grass. It ended at the mouth of the open grave. He moved closer. There, six feet down, at the bottom of the human-sized hole that bore the bite marks of Daisy's backhoe, was a black mass of cloak. He stifled a scream, swallowing his own soul back into his body before one of the envious dead grabbed it.

Something kept him rooted to the lip of the open grave. Something that had been ingrained in him for a short, but no less, a lifetime of experience with dead bodies. Douglas knew the stillness at the bottom of that shaft.

The monster had landed on the concrete grave liner, the black smear on the snow-covered lip testifying to where his head had hit. A head that was now completely slipped of its black hood.

The monster in that grave wasn't the Grim Reaper. In the light of Daisy's headlamps, he could see that the killer's extremely pale head was bald except for a thin fringe of light blond hair around the temples. He had a moustache that was the same color, and a pair of round spectacles that were askew on his face.

The man at the photo booth at the Cowlmouth Fall Carnival.

The monster, the murderer, was an ordinary man. A coffee-drinker. And he was somewhere that he wasn't a danger to anybody, exactly like Douglas's father had hoped for. It was the only corpse Douglas had ever seen that didn't look at peace.

As the snow slowly buried the body in white, three shapes quickly detached from the mottled mist behind him. Douglas smelled cloves, heard the jangle of keys on chains, and felt a skinny arm covered in a tattered sweater slip around his shoulders.

"Have I ever told you, Spadeful," one of the shapes said breathlessly through a rasp of beard, "that holes are the best things in the entire world?"

November 14

MONDAY

CHAPTER
25

Now this was a merry funeral. Douglas hung back in the empty foyer of Cowlmouth Center Church and watched the festivities in the auditorium through the crack where the two doors met. People were wearing brightly colored party hats instead of somber veils, burying their faces in glasses of punch instead of into handkerchiefs. In lieu of memorial funeral programs, people hefted small paper plates piled with cheeses and meats and olives and other foods that could be skewered by toothpicks. Napkins were stuffed into collars and worn down the front of shirts in place of ties. What would normally have been a muted, respectful buzz of conversation had moved up the ladder to a boisterous roar. The crowd was huge, bigger even than the one at Mr. Stauffer's funeral had been. The attendees—the anti-mourners—weren't sitting somberly in ordered rows, either. They were milling about excitedly, clumped in animated clusters among the pews.

Douglas's eyes roamed the sliver of crowd that he could see through the crack. He was looking for somebody specific, but all he could see was the almost solid mass of people wandering under the blind, bemused gaze of the blue-and-white stained glass window behind the pulpit. Every once in a while, the open coffin at the front of the auditorium was visible through breaks in the crowd.

"Let me see." Lowell lightly pushed Douglas away from the doors and stuck his face to the crevice. Had somebody pushed the door from the opposite side, Lowell would have earned a black eye that would've stuck around until Christmas. He was wearing jeans and a long-sleeved gray pullover. A faded red stripe slithered down the length of each sleeve, which stopped short a good inch before his bony wrists. "Man . . . everybody's in there."

"Everybody?" asked Douglas.

Before Lowell could answer, the outside doors

behind them opened, and in swept a rush of cold November air accompanied by two men who walked gently into the foyer like they didn't trust the carpet under their snow-encrusted boots. Moss and Feaster both wore beat-up jackets, Moss's of brown tweed and Feasters of green suede. Moss's shirt was buttoned all the way to his beard, and Feaster had a rudimentary part in his hair that looked more like a ragged scar than a neat division. In fact, the pair almost looked like imposters of Moss and Feaster, especially since neither one of them hoisted a shovel or leaned on a pickax. It was like they both had suffered amputations.

It had been two weeks since the four of them stood together in the snow at that impromptu funeral service. Two weeks since Halloween. Two weeks since the dark burden of Cowlmouth had rolled right off its back and into an open grave.

"I don't remember the last time I saw you at a funeral service." Douglas wasn't sure about calling it that.

"Eh," dismissed Feaster with a wave of a hand that was remarkably clean except for the dark edges of his fingernails. "We get our time with the dead, you know that. But we figured this was a special occasion."

"So how are you two doing?" asked Moss, scratching

uncomfortably at a beard that seemed to have been lavished with a scented cream strong enough to fight a violent battle with Feaster's aroma of cloves.

"Okay, I guess," Douglas answered for both of them.

"I bet you guys are," replied Feaster. "I bet you're more than okay. We got real heroes, here, Moss, you know." Douglas felt warmth fill his face.

"Bona fide monster slayers," agreed Moss.

"Fellow monster slayers," corrected Feaster.

"It was all Doug," protested Lowell. "I never even really saw the creep. At least, while he was alive."

"He fell into a hole." Douglas felt as if he had offered that explanation a thousand times in the past two weeks. Nobody seemed to listen to it.

"Don't matter how you did it. Matters that you did it," said Moss, twisting his neck uncomfortably and reaching under his beard to unfasten one of his shirt buttons. "We're just sorry we weren't there to help you." They had already apologized too many times to Douglas for taking a break from cemetery business to enjoy Halloween in town for a bit.

"No good ever comes from us leaving that boneyard," said Feaster. He tugged at the uneven ponytail that he'd gathered his long, brown hair into.

"Still," said Moss, "It's good to know that when we're gone, there'll be somebody here who can take care of Cowlmouth's monsters. We're getting old, you know."

"Speak for yourself," said Feaster, "You always forget that you've got decades on me."

"A few years, sure."

"Decades," Feaster insisted. "I'll be throwing dirt on your box before I've even hit my prime."

"We'll see. The fickle Fates cut strange expiration dates."

Feaster shrugged at the old argument and turned back to Douglas and Lowell. "You're going to want know that we had to fix the lock on the Grassley mausoleum. Too many people poking around it after your story got out."

"But we left another one open for you elsewhere in the cemetery," said Moss with a wink that made one side of his beard twitch. "We'll leave it to you to find it. Make sure you keep it secret from us."

"Thanks," said Douglas distractedly as his eyes were again drawn to the thin stripe of activity between the doors.

"Why aren't you going in there?" asked Moss.

Douglas looked down at his dress shoes. He'd shined

them that morning and could see his reflection looking up at himself. It was disconcerting and made him feel like he was falling. "I don't know."

"Looks like a real party," urged Feaster.

"Where are your folks?" asked Moss.

"Already in there. Came over early to help set everything up. Said we could come over whenever we felt like it."

"Feels good to be able to walk the streets of Cowlmouth by yourselves again, eh?" asked Feaster.

"Yeah," agreed Douglas. It really was.

"Too bad this will probably be our last time for a while. We're both grounded until Thanksgiving," said Lowell.

"What?" said Feaster, "Heroes such as yourselves?"

"Our parents didn't like us keeping things from them and putting ourselves in danger," said Douglas. He'd almost gotten away with a sentence of extra funeral home duties, but then his parents remembered that he liked doing that kind of stuff. So, grounded it was. Until *at least* Thanksgiving.

"Well," said Moss, who had managed to undo another two buttons of his shirt and had twisted an arm halfway out of his jacket. "No reason for you to be spending your last moments of freedom with us anti-social types. I'm sure there are lots of people waiting for you guys in there."

"I guess," replied Douglas feebly while gently dabbing at the three stripes of hair on his forehead.

"You need a push?" asked Feaster.

"Nope. We're going in." Lowell grabbed Douglas by the arm and pulled him through the doors like he was delivering an order at a restaurant. Douglas didn't protest.

The crowd barely parted as the two boys stepped into the noisy auditorium. Douglas had received so much attention lately that he had expected—and dreaded—everybody making a big commotion when he arrived. Thankfully, the crowd was too big and having too much fun to notice such a small detail as two more in their midst. The only eye staring at them was the giant pupilless one at the front of the church.

The walls of the auditorium were covered in rainbows of brightly-colored streamers, and the ends of the pews were topped with large bows. Off to the side of the church, at a respectable distance away from the open coffin, was a large TV that cycled through images of Lavinia Laurent, Marvin Brinsfield, and George

Rivets. Nearby, Douglas saw his parents talking to Dr. Coffman and Chief Pumphrey. It was a grouping that usually meant that the details of a death needed sorting, but this time, they were all smiling and eating and not acting like any one of them had ever seen a dead body in their entire lives. Douglas's father saw him and gave him a quick wink. His father, the mortician, who had seen plenty of dead bodies, who had helped plenty of living people get through death so that they could go back to living.

"Hail, Dorothies!" The voice came from his left, and was followed by Eddie Brunswick, who sauntered over to him with a glass of punch in his even-fingered hand and a plate of deviled eggs in his other. His brown shirt bore his average number of stains.

"Dad really needs to invest in more smocks for you," Douglas said.

"Doesn't matter. If it weren't mortuary fluids, it'd be food stains." The way the level of punch seesawed in the glass and the deviled eggs wobbled on the plate seemed to support the statement.

"Whoa," said Lowell. "Deviled eggs? Where at?"

Eddie thrust his glass in the general direction of a wall at the far end of the church. "Full buffet."

"I've got high standards for *full*," insisted Lowell. "I'll catch up with you guys," and like that Lowell was lost in the crowd.

"How's the funeral going?" asked Douglas.

"I've been to better ones. Haven't been to a better party, though." He took a sip from his glass and smiled, his teeth red from the liquid. "It's crazy, man. I guarantee you every conversation in this church is about murder, yet I haven't seen so many smiles in my entire life." He paused. "Hey, shouldn't you get announced or something? You're like the guest of honor at this thing. The most famous person in Cowlmouth."

"He fell into a hole."

"Ha," said Eddie, but not in response to Douglas's statement. He was waving his glass haphazardly in the direction of a back corner of the church. "There's Chris. I thought that guy would never go near a funeral again." Douglas hadn't seen Christopher in more than a month, since the last—the actual last—murder. He was wearing black jeans and a burgundy sweater. The thin growth of hair on his upper lip had spread to his chin. Chris looked very different from how Douglas was used to seeing him, in the somber suits of the trade. He also looked a lot more relaxed. Nevertheless, he was about as far away from the coffin as he could physically be and still share an auditorium with it.

"You know what he's doing these days?" asked Eddie.

"No," answered Douglas without interest, as he continued to scan the crowd.

"Accountant. First the death biz, then the tax biz. Ha. Wants a sure thing, that guy."

"He was just never really cut out for death," said Douglas, noncommittally.

"Nonsense," replied Eddie, a little too loudly. "Everybody's cut out for death. I haven't stitched together a single stiff who wasn't extremely good at being dead." *Stiff* wasn't exactly proper funeral terminology, but Douglas doubted that Eddie would have been reprimanded this time if his father had overheard him. "When it comes to dying, we're all professionals. Maybe one day I'll get to be his embalmer. Then I'll tell him, 'I told you so.'"

Douglas nodded and attempted to excuse himself, but took half a step into a golden crucifix on the end of a chain.

"Nice tie," said a voice above the crucifix. The tie was light blue.

Reverend Ahlgrim wasn't wearing a party hat and he wasn't carrying around any food or drink. For once, he actually looked out of place in his own church.

"How are you doing, son? I was wondering if you were around."

"I'm okay. There's a party hat on Jesus."

The pastor turned his round head around to look at the large wooden messiah hanging on the back wall of the church. A bright green conical hat had been perched slightly askew on the upturned head of the savior. The reverend sighed and Eddie let out a loud laugh. "So there is. I suppose that's blasphemy. I really should have made the balconies off-limits. But I have to assume that Christ celebrates with us when good triumphs over evil."

He fell into a hole. Douglas nodded.

"Are you looking for your parents?"

"No."

"That's good. I couldn't help you if you were. I don't think we've ever had this many people here. Certainly not this many people carrying around food and drink. The Lord will have to work one of his miracles for the carpets, I'm afraid." The reverend took off his glasses and started rubbing the round lenses with a cloth that he pulled from his pants pocket. "I'm glad the town's picking up the cleaning bill for the mess."

At that moment, Douglas caught a glimpse of the coffin through a random shift in the crowd. "Yeah, well, I think I'm going pay my respects." He walked backward a few steps, as the reverend scolded Eddie for how dangerously close to spilling his glass he was. Eddie ignored him and exclaimed, "Is that Moss and Feaster? At a funeral?" Douglas spun around and headed to the coffin.

As he jostled past reveler after reveler, he caught a brief glimpse of a tall woman in glasses wearing a red dress covered in large, white, wide-petaled flowers—Ms. Basford. She stared coldly at him. It seems like it would take more than a dead murderer to win her over to his way of life. He nodded his head at her and hurried his pace.

The Splendor 4000 looked especially grand in its new context, outside of the showroom, in the dead spot of the church, with no other coffins around fighting for attention. The gold-rubbed wood almost glowed beneath the soft church lighting. The entire full-couch lid of the coffin was thrown open to reveal a sumptuous lining of pale, padded Chinese silk. A few others stood at the coffin, gazing fixedly into its interior like there was a television screen inside.

Now that Douglas was beside it, he was less interested in the casket than what was inside. Three objects sat incongruously in the lush silk interior. The first was a black, hooded cloak, laid out like a body would have been, the empty hood resting on the richly embroidered coffin pillow. The second item was a long, thin knife, laid atop the cloak. Now that Douglas saw both of these items in the full light of the church, without anybody wearing the one or holding the other, they didn't look so terrifying.

The third item was a newspaper, folded in half and placed beside the knife like a dinner setting. The headline was black and stark, like the dark robe against the ivory silk.

SERIAL KILLER DIES CHASING LOCAL YOUTHS

It could easily have been, SERIAL KILLER MURDERS LOCAL YOUTHS, Douglas knew. As it was, the headline was the opposite of an epitaph, and that's why the funeral was such a party. They were celebrating a different kind of end. The killer's body, his parents had told him, had been donated to science, although some of the unwanted bits had been buried in an unmarked plot somewhere secret in Cowlmouth Cemetery. Moss and Feaster were the only ones who knew where.

Douglas had read this particular newspaper article about a hundred times online and had a copy of the archaic two-week-old paper version in his bedroom on top of a pile of about two dozen other articles printed in the town paper that talked about the story. A few of them even included quotes from him. There wasn't much to this particular article, though, since it was the first. Just the fact of the serial killer's death and that it involved the son of a local funeral home director and the son of the town's police chief.

Later articles went into more detail . . . as much as there was, anyway. Nothing was ever discovered about the Family Man, which was the new name that the press had posthumously given the serial killer. He had no identification on him, nobody recognized him. Even the company that had hired him for the carnival knew nothing about him. The identification he had used to get the job turned out to be fake. The news went national, and still nobody came forward with any useful information. He was apparently a man without a family, which was perhaps why he was building one in Cowlmouth. Because he had been using Death House as a hideout, another rumor had him as a descendent of the family that was killed there. That he was recreating the family that he had lost. That was probably the story that would stick among the kids in town, the story that would be passed along on every Halloween and to every generation. "Beware the Family Man . . . He's always hunting for new additions to his family."

Douglas lost interest in the contents of the casket quicker than he had lost interest in the casket itself. He started threading his way through the crowd in the direction that Lowell had taken. It was slow going since every other person wanted to shake his hand or talk to him about that night in the graveyard. He did the former as quickly as he could, gently protested the latter, and in that slow manner, finally made it to the food, which was set atop a line of folding tables covered in white table cloths against the wall of the church.

He saw Lowell first, two plates in his hands and his cheeks chipmunked full of who-knew-what. It took him only a few heartbeats more to see Audrey. Her back was toward him. She was wearing a thick orange sweater, and her dark hair was loose about her shoulders. Before

Douglas quite made it to her, she turned around, a small paper plate in her hand, the purple stone of her ring standing out among the bright red strawberries resting there. The last time he had seen her, a large white bandage had been taped to her cheek to cover up the stitches from where the killer's knife had grazed her. Today, the bandage and the stitches were gone, revealing a short, thin arc of a scar. It looked like the blade of a scythe. In a few weeks, it would barely be noticeable.

As soon as she saw Douglas, she put her plate down on the table and ran to him, throwing her arms around his neck. He couldn't feel the scar pressing into his own cheek.

It felt good. And he was only a little embarrassed.

ACKNOWLEDGMENTS

When I started to write this story, my oldest daughter was an infant. By the time it got published, she'd aged into its target audience. Over the course of those many years in between, a few people really supported and cared for this book. My wife, Lindsey, was the very first. The first to read it. The first to show excitement for it. The first to encourage me about it. Next came Christian Haunton, whose insights and advice elevated this book to a place beyond the limits of my own instincts. It was only after his suggestions that this book stood a chance. After Christian came Bethany Buck, whose tireless efforts on its behalf are the only reason why this book isn't still trapped on my hard drive today. I cannot understate her role in this book's publication. Finally, Alison Weiss came along and shouldered it through the hard publication home-stretch, caring for it as her own despite adverse circumstances, and finding further ways to improve it.

All to make a strange boy in an ill-fitting suit live and almost die and live.

Douglas and I thank all of you.